TEACH ME TO LOVE

TEACH ME TO LOVE

BROTHERS OF BELLE FOURCHE: BOOK 1

KARI TRUMBO

PRAISE FOR TEACH ME TO LOVE

"Kari Trumbo's decisive writing gives this dialogue a realistic feel in a historical setting. Teach Me To Love is an intense read which will keep you entertained for a couple hours. The charisma between the characters allows the reader to grow with them."

~Wend Jo Wipf for Readers' Favorite

"I loved this book. It was very hard for me to put down. The writing was fantastic and the characters! The characters were wonderfully written."

~JoAnn B. Amazon Reviewer

"This was a truly moving story about Izzy a young woman who has suffered mental abuse at the hands of her husband. The storyline flowed beautifully [with] action and drama but the fundamental feeling I had whilst listening to this story was one of wellbeing and love…"

~Amazon Reviewer

To those who are mourning:

[11]You have turned my mourning into dancing for me. You have removed my sackcloth, and clothed me with gladness, [12]To the end that my heart may sing praise to you, and not be silent. Yahweh my God, I will give thanks to you forever! Psalm 30:11-12

PROLOGUE

Tinton, South Dakota
May 1899

I t wasn't right to pray he would just die. Yet her wicked heart screamed the words she'd learned to swallow over the last year. Her husband, Harland Lawson, was sick with some vile disease he'd picked up from the bordello, and it took more energy to build up sympathy for him than it took to scrub the floor spotless.

"Get in here, you fat monstrosity!" he croaked from his bed.

Izzy bit her lip to keep from saying anything. He'd never hit her before, but broken her with his words, telling her—and anyone who would listen—all her faults, including her most intimate ones.

"You need to get your family here. They'll take care of me. You're good for nothing. Never were. Your ma would do right by me, she'd make sure I had good food to eat."

The truth of his words burned deeply. Her parents would side with him. They'd liked him, doted on him, loved him.

The one time she'd tried to tell her mother about Harland and his treatment, her mother wouldn't listen, saying all new marriages had troubles. It was just growing pains.

"I won't bother my family over you. I won't bother with you. Lie in the bed you made, Harland Lawson." It was the closest she'd come to speaking her mind in so long, her whole body tensed under the stress.

"You're nothing without me. You can't teach, because you didn't finish school. You can't catch another man, because you're too big. You can't do anything."

Those words had long since lost their sting. She knew she was *big,* and she had sold every mirror in their home, except for Harland's shaving mirror, to avoid the visual truth of his words. They didn't own much of anything anymore, she'd had to sell it all when he took sick.

"When you die, I won't miss you. *No one* will miss you. At least I can go to Lula's." She stood back from the bed; even weak, he frightened her. He knew her every weakness, and with a few words, could usually bring her to tears.

"I forbid you to go anywhere near that woman! She's got notions!"

Anger sparked deep and hot in her heart, and she refused to be silent a moment longer. "Go to Hell, Harland."

CHAPTER 1

Belle Fourche, South Dakota
June 1899

For the first time in two days, Izzy had doubts as she rode along the hilly trail. During the last year and a half, she hadn't been allowed to see anyone, nor make a single decision. Now that she had to decide what to do with her life, she was thoroughly out of practice. Harland had died two days before, leaving her nothing but a burning ache for freedom and a sickness in her gut at the thought of him.

Her only other option had been her dearest friend from school, Lula Oleson, who was now married and living on a ranch in Belle Fourche. It was the very place she needed to find. She and Lula had corresponded often. However, the full truth of what she'd been living with would be so harsh, Izzy had feared telling Lula. What could Lula have done, anyway, besides worry? It wasn't like Izzy could just divorce Harland, he wouldn't have allowed it, and it wouldn't have been right. Decisions had consequences, and hers had cost her dearly.

Her horse nickered, and she jumped. In the distance, she could just make out two poles with an arched sign between them. The post master in Belle Fourche had told her when she saw it, she was almost to the Oleson place. The Broken Circle O, which was owned by Barton and his older brothers, was her destination. Izzy breathed a deep sigh, *soon*. Lula would be there, and for the first time in the longest eighteen months of her life, she'd get an embrace from someone who wanted her. She'd be somewhere she could sit for a few minutes and rest. Guilt ate at her for not feeling a lick of sadness over losing her husband, but she'd long since lost all warm feelings where he was concerned.

The upright posts were close enough now that she could see the brand with the large O and another circle around it, which was missing a piece in the upper right of the circle. The brand and name sat in the center of a curved sign above the wide entrance. She said a prayer that they would be welcoming, but she'd said a lot of prayers over the last several months. All seemed to have fallen on deaf ears. A rider on a chestnut horse rode toward her at an easy pace, obviously not concerned by her approach. He had a relaxed look about him and his shoulders swayed along to the gait of the horse.

She waved a welcome, and he nodded but continued toward her. Her stomach did a little flip. It had been so long since she'd dealt with another person. Would he judge her just as Harland always had? Too late to turn back now. As he neared her, her body tensed. She couldn't see much about him besides his wide shoulders and easy seat in the saddle. In the summer heat, he wore brown trousers and a loose linen shirt with a white undershirt. It was possible he'd spent more time on his horse than on his own two feet. The man wasn't Lula's husband, Barton, and he wasn't old enough to be

4

Barton's pa, so he had to be one of his brothers. She'd secretly hoped she'd make it all the way to Lula before she was discovered by anyone else so she wouldn't have to face anyone. Harland had taught her quickly that men couldn't be trusted. He'd been so kind at first.

The jittery feeling turned to a buzzing in her head. The heat had gotten to her on the last leg of her journey. Her canteen had run out and she'd been loath to stop. Discomfort had been her companion for so long, what was another day? So, even when her tongue felt as thick as a feather tick, she hadn't stopped to replenish. Now, as the land around her seemed to undulate with the heat, she wished she had.

The man reined in a few yards from her and she likewise left space between them. Now she could see his face, though it was shadowed under his dark Stetson. He had a strong jaw, high cheekbones, and hard eyes. If she let herself, she could almost imagine he'd be just as handsome as his brother Barton, if he smiled. He shifted in the saddle and stared at her for a few moments longer than she expected. Was he judging her even now?

"I..." It felt so strange to speak without being given permission. "I'm Izzy Lawson and I'm here to see Lula Oleson."

He nodded, his lips remaining a hard, dark slash under his wide hat brim. It would be so much easier to speak to him—so much less intimidating—if he weren't hidden beneath his cover.

He turned his horse around and glanced at her over his broad shoulder. "Conrad Oleson. I'll show you up to the house."

WHAT KIND of a name was *Izzy*? Conrad kept his back straight in the saddle and wouldn't let himself glance back at the scrawny woman behind him. She'd tucked her head and barely looked up at him anyway. What he *had* noticed was her lightly curled hair had bleached and looked almost faded in the sun, but it was a warm brown where the sun hadn't touched it. Her eyes were a gentle blue. Lula had never mentioned an Izzy to him that he could recall, but she had so many sisters, it was difficult to remember all their names.

"Are you one of Lula's sisters?" He offered over his shoulder. Her lack of conversation was strange to say the least. Weren't most women-folk ones to talk your ears off? It was one of the reasons he'd never bothered with finding one. He didn't like the chatter. Not to mention, the only girls he'd ever had occasion to meet had been at school, and since he'd been a less-than-fine student, none of the young ladies had paid him much mind. That had been over eleven years ago, not that he thought about it… overmuch.

Her voice was soft, raspy. As if she struggled to get her words out. "No, sir. I'm a friend from the Spearfish school."

Tension coiled in his gut. Another teacher. As if having two of the insufferable breed around weren't enough. Lula had tried often to pressure him into reading. Either to prove to herself that he could read, or couldn't. She needed to have *someone* to teach. He'd been a little project for her ever since she'd gotten in a family way and the school board released her of her teaching duties. She was probably under the direction of his meddlesome little brother, Barton. It wasn't anyone's business if he could read or not, and this new tiny teacher could go right back to where she came from if Lula had invited her there just to force him into giving up his secret.

Back in grade school, reading had been difficult. He could

never seem to make the right sounds with the right letters. It had been so difficult, in fact, he'd given up ever learning, and there wasn't time now anyway. He was needed every day, at all hours, to work the ranch. No matter how much it might help matters, he couldn't make the time to learn.

He pulled to a stop, slipped his canteen from its pouch, and spun off the top, leaning toward her to hand it off. The woman looked plum parched and he suspected the canteen dangling from her saddle was long dry. She leaned back for a moment, eyeing it, then gave in and took a long pull. She wiped her mouth with the back of her arm and handed it back to him, though she still eyed him like a dog that had been whipped. It cut at him in a place deeper than his heart, and he shoved the feeling away. The teacher wasn't going to stay. He wouldn't let her.

"Thank you." She seemed to shrink in on herself the closer he got to her and wouldn't keep her eyes on him.

"You a teacher, then?" He ground out the words. He disliked teachers, but this one seemed pretty harmless.

She hesitated. Her voice so quiet he had to strain to hear. "No, sir."

"But, didn't you say you were from the Normal School?" Why couldn't the woman just answer and be done with it? Did every teacher have to try to be sneaky?

"I was, but I didn't finish. I was married instead."

He held his breath for a moment and waited until she looked back up at him. "If you're married, where's your husband?"

Her soft blue eyes turned hard, and cold, the little golden flecks at their center like fire from within. "I hope he's in hell," she whispered, her shoulders shuddered as she looked away yet again.

A pretty blush crept up her neck and turned her cheeks,

already pink with the sun, a deep rose. What was a woman doing riding all alone after losing her husband, and what had the man done to make her hate him so? By the way she refused to look him in the eye for longer than a breath, and how quiet she'd been, he got the distinct feeling that she was unused to speaking her mind. That was so very different from every teacher he'd ever known. He waited, but she didn't say more, and for once, he wished she would.

"The house is just up yonder. Lula and Barton live on their own place, but he leaves her at the house every day, so that's where she'll be."

"Thank you, sir. You've been most kind."

No, he hadn't. He wasn't fool enough to believe such nonsense and he had to clench his teeth to keep from correcting her. While her dander had been up when he'd mentioned her mister, she was generally placid, and something about that bothered him. A woman wasn't supposed to be. She was supposed to smile and bring warmth and noise, and bring a man to smile even if he didn't want to. This woman seemed to have forgotten how to do any of that, and deep inside, he couldn't shake the question, *why?*

"I'll take your horse to the barn and bring your saddle bag back up later." He pulled to a stop and dismounted, flipping the rein over the saddle horn, confident Talon wouldn't move anyway. He stepped around Mrs. Lawson's horse, just as Mrs. Lawson rose up to dismount. She'd been riding astride, and he'd just noticed her booted feet sticking out from her skirts when her eyes rolled back into her head and her body went limp. He groped for her waist and tugged her down toward him so she didn't fall under the horse's hooves.

Fool woman. Felt like she weighed less than a sack of oats. Why did women have to be so tiny? They never seemed to tire of telling men to eat, couldn't they take a minute to listen to their own advice?

Her head lolled against his shoulder, her soft hair tickling his chin. It was the first time he'd had a woman in his arms, and the weight of her pressed against him ignited a need deep inside his chest to keep watch over the slip of a woman. He made it up the front porch steps and tried to open the screen door.

"Mama! Can you come let me in?" he called, trying not to fumble Mrs. Lawson. He didn't want to jostle her, but he couldn't reach the door handle.

Dainty booted feet rushed toward him as his mother appeared, a kitchen towel draped over her shoulder, and she paused to wipe her hands on her long apron. His mama was four foot nothing, but what she lacked in height, she made up for in spunk. Her chocolate brown hair, streaked with silver, was tied back into a loose bun, which looked like it would fall out at any moment but never did. The ranch wouldn't be half the home it was without her.

"Good gracious, Conrad. Who've you got there?" She shoved open the door and held it wide so he could sidle on in. Lula lumbered into the room under the weight of her widening waistline.

She gasped. "Izzy!" Lula cried out, her hand flying to her mouth, her eyes wide in her suddenly pale face. "Lay her on the couch! Where did you find her, Conrad?"

He hadn't found her, she'd found him. At least that's how it seemed. "She was riding up when I was leaving for town. I brought her back, seemed like the right thing to do."

Manners weren't his biggest strength. Mama had told him so, but it was a good thing he'd followed his gut this time, or Mrs. Lawson would've ended up in the dirt and might not have been found until the next person went to town.

"What's the matter with her?" He peered over Lula's shoulder.

Lula laid the back of her hand over Mrs. Lawson's forehead then brushed the hair from her face. He should leave the room, it wasn't his place to be here. But, Mrs. Lawson sure was pretty when her face was relaxed. If she wasn't so wary, so frightened to speak up and look him in the eye, she'd be hard to ignore. But right now, he couldn't let himself harbor any such thoughts. There was more wrong with her than right. She was far too skinny, almost sickly. Her skin was thin and she was pale. Her lips were the only plump curve he could find, and he didn't mind looking at them one bit.

"Oh, Izzy. What's happened to you?" Lula mumbled. Conrad couldn't help but wonder the same thing.

CHAPTER 2

The scent of roses. Why could Izzy smell roses? She forced her eyes open. Harland wouldn't even let her buy scented soap... Lula's face hovered over hers. She'd made it. Lula's rose scented hand reached down and clasped hers as a tear fell from Lula's cheek.

"What did he do to you? Why didn't you tell me in your letters, dear Izzy?" Lula drew Izzy's hand to her chest and held it there tightly. "He was a monster, wasn't he? A dreadful monster."

What could Izzy have said? Her own parents hadn't believed her. Harland's treatment had been within their sight and they'd done nothing. How would Lula have believed her in a letter? Not to mention what might have befallen her if Harland had discovered what she'd done. Most of the damage Harland had wrought could be fixed, with time. Izzy squeezed her eyes shut, pushing away the flood of pain once again. She wouldn't drown now that she was free.

"It isn't anything." She pushed herself to sit up and the edges of her vision darkened, pushing her back against the arm of the couch. Izzy took a deep breath and tried to focus on Lula.

"Isn't anything? Have you looked in a mirror lately? You're skin and bones. Don't try and tell me this wasn't Harland's fault. I heard what he said about you in class after you married him." She stood up and paced to one end of the room and back again, the blonde ringlets that had fallen from her bun bouncing with every movement. Quite a feat in her large state. Lula never paced, it drove her crazy, yet she was quivering with fury.

"You needn't worry about him anymore. He died. Days ago." Izzy couldn't believe how easy it was to say the words, and she couldn't even remember the exact number of days it had been now.

Lula spun and faced her. "He died? How? Better question… how did you get here?" Lula strode back to her and sat, regarding her with those intense blue eyes. She'd almost forgotten what it was like to sit and talk to a friend, to confide in anyone. How had she lived so long without Lula, her most dear friend?

"About the only thing Harland didn't sell to pay for rent was his horse. So, I took it. I don't know who paid for his burial…and I don't care. I know I should be ashamed, but I'm not. He was a horrible man. I still haven't figured out what he ever saw in me or why he wanted to marry me. He was dissatisfied from the very start. After you told me what he'd said in class—that I was too *big* under all my underthings—I told him what I thought of his talking about me. After that, he didn't even pretend to care." The cold tone of her own accounting made her shiver, it was like she spoke of someone else's life, not her own.

Izzy stopped, took a breath, then finished. "The day of

your wedding was the last time I went out on my own. He didn't want anyone to see me after that."

Utter shock and pain crossed Lula's sweet face. "How can that be? Didn't you go to the store? How could he just keep you inside…like a prisoner?"

Heat rushed up her cheeks. Every time she thought about what he'd done, she felt like someone's misbehaving child, not a wife.

"He told me if I left the apartment, he wouldn't allow me to eat for one whole day. He would stay home or have people from town watch me and make sure I didn't. We always lived above a store or another house, so the people below would know if I tried to leave."

Even now that it was over, she couldn't stop from wringing her hands as she told the tale. He'd controlled her every movement. Her heart raced as though he'd walk through the door and hit her with his foul words once again, just for speaking ill of him.

"I suffered through a whole summer with various, creative punishments. I prayed for the school year to start so he could begin his internship and I would have a measure of freedom from him. Except, he didn't get it. He was turned away. We went to Tinton where he heard they were looking for a teacher. He only worked there for about six months when the school board fired him."

"Fired him?" Lula slid forward in her seat. "You don't have to talk if you don't want to. Let's get you a little bite to eat and let you rest." She patted Izzy's hand, and though she didn't want to speak of it, she had to tell someone, to share her burden, or she might burst.

"I was pregnant, Lula," Izzy choked. She'd never told anyone. The precious life had long dried up, but she hadn't been able to

13

bear speaking about it before, and she needed comfort from someone. Seeing Lula with her rounded waist ripped open the ache. "When I told him, I thought he'd be happy, that he would *finally* love me. Or, at the least, would love the babe." The burn of tears strained against her eyes, but no moisture would come.

"Instead, he went to the whorehouse and got herbs to take care of it. He put them in my food and didn't tell me until after I'd eaten." Her sob was so powerful it nearly broke her, but her eyes remained dry. "I should have known when he encouraged me to eat. I should've been suspicious. He *never* wanted me to eat. Why didn't I see it, Lula?" The guilt she'd placed on her own shoulders weighed all the heavier after her admission.

Lula pressed her rose scented kerchief into Izzy's hand. Izzy patted at her eyes with an automatic motion, but no tears came. "After that, his punishments didn't bother me. I never wanted to eat again, anyway. I think part of my heart died along with the precious baby."

Lula pressed her tiny hands to Izzy's cheeks. "Now, you listen to me. I'm so sorry for all the things he did to you. I knew he was awful, but I never would've guessed he'd go so far as to kill his own child. You're here now, and you're safe. We'll take care of you."

Izzy's stomach rumbled, and she jumped at the strange noise. It had been so long since she'd allowed herself to even think about food. The last few months, she'd only eaten because she had to in order to stay alive... Even then, though, she wondered at the time why she bothered.

"Rest now. I'll bring you in a tray."

Rest. That was exactly what she needed.

CONRAD STOOD IN THE STABLE, waiting for his wrangler, Stan, to show up. He was always late, but he was the best Conrad had ever seen with the horses. Conrad had fed and watered Talon and the bay and white Pinto Mrs. Lawson had rode in on and now he had nothing to do. The horse now stood content in its stall, its head and neck relaxed. It might even be sleeping, not that he'd go over and check. It had been ridden a long time, at least from the sheen of sweat shining on his coat, and obviously, so had Mrs. Lawson. Where had she come from? And why?

He'd never been so curious about a woman before. Granted, this one had landed right in his arms, and that didn't happen every day.

Stan trudged into the opposite end of the barn, his legs permanently bowed from a life spent on a horse, and his hat a little too floppy to do much good.

"Boss. What you be needin'?"

The lazy way Stan spoke made Conrad's ears ring and he gritted his teeth. "I need about five extra ropers for the next month. Pay is a dollar a day, no more."

Stan leaned against a wide beam, a slow smile crept over rotten and missing teeth. "Want me to write up the contracts?"

The evil gleam in Stan's eye shot right to Conrad's heart. There was no way Conrad could write up the contract himself. The only one who probably could was Barton, and he'd never ask his little brother to do it.

"Just get them here. They don't need to be under contract. It's only a month."

"What if they ask for one?" Stan narrowed his eyes and waited. Conrad hated feeling trapped, but if Stan knew for sure he couldn't read, he might take advantage. While he was good with horses, he wasn't a good man.

"Then they don't need a job." He turned on his heel. Stan had recently left him feeling agitated at every turn. He'd need to find someone else to work with soon.

"Whose horse is that? Don't recognize it."

A chill drove up Conrad's back. Mrs. Lawson didn't need to worry about the wrangler coming anywhere near her, and Stan might make it a point to be bothersome.

"Just a visitor for Barton's wife. None of your concern."

Stan laughed and headed back the way he came. The time to replace Stan was fast approaching. It would have to be done when he could manage to find the time to look for another wrangler who was good enough. They had so many horses they couldn't go without, not even for a day.

Now that his meeting with Stan was over, he wandered back up to the house, which really wasn't his place. He only came back to the house for family supper on Sunday, but Mrs. Lawson was a curiosity, one his other brothers hadn't discovered yet.

He peered through the door and saw her tiny feet still propped up against the end of the couch. She was still lying where he'd left her. Was she awake? He pulled the door open and sneaked inside, careful not to make any noise. Her eyes were closed, with a dark ribbon of lashes sweeping over her cheeks. There was an empty plate next to her. Praise the Lord, she'd eaten something. It would take more than one plate to get her looking fit again, though.

His feet shuffled quietly over the floor as he made his way over to her. What had brought her out to the Broken Circle O, and would she stay? As he sat in the chair facing the couch, it groaned under his weight and her blue eyes slid open. They widened for just a moment and she sucked in air as if she might scream as she backed as far into the couch as she could.

He had to stop her before she sent the whole house running. "Don't be scared. You met me on the road, remember?" He knew he was muscled and a little rangy, and with a life of hard work and his ma's good cooking, he could be a mite scary.

Her shoulders relaxed slightly as she took in every inch of his face, the wariness slipping away slowly. He liked the way she took her time to look him over and didn't try to hide it. So many women hid behind fans or pretended to never really look at anything, but Mrs. Lawson fairly inspected him.

"I didn't remember, but now I do. My mind is still a little sleep muddled." She didn't raise her head from the couch, and he would've told her not to bother if she had.

He couldn't keep from staring at her, until she closed her eyes and heat rose up her cheeks.

He averted his eyes to his hands in his lap. "I'm sorry. I don't mean to be so bold. My mama tells me I have the worst manners."

He glanced back into her eyes and she returned it, reaching for his hand and lightly patting the top of his knuckles. "I assure you, your manners are impeccable compared to what I'm used to. Thank you, sir." Her gentle touch left a lingering heat against his skin, like the warmth of the summer sun.

"Please don't call me sir; it doesn't seem to fit me. Appears like you're practically family to Lula, so why don't you just call me Conrad, like everyone else?"

"I hardly know you." She turned her face away, the red in her cheeks deepening.

"If we were in some stuffy drawing room, or even in town where people would hear, I'd agree with you. But no one out here will care, they all know my name. We are a bit...

unconventional out here." And the faster he did away with formalities, the faster he could learn more about this strange, lovely woman.

Izzy looked up at him, her chin to her chest. "Well, if we are to completely flout convention, then you must call me Izzy. I was married, so it isn't as if I'm not used to it. Not to mention, I rather hate the name Lawson."

He'd have to find out what her husband had done to make this beauty hate him so. But not today. He stood, ready to let her get more rest, and watched as her shoulders slumped in exhaustion.

"Well, there you have it. Someday, I'll ask you what Izzy stands for."

"That's an easy question to answer." She sighed as she made herself comfortable on the couch once again, stretching her toes languidly and arranging the blanket. "I am Isabelle Rosemary. It was good to meet you, Conrad, and thank you for making sure I got to the house. The last thing I remember is trying to dismount from Mule. I was just so tired."

Now it was his turn to get hot under the collar. She didn't remember he'd carried her in the house, and he wasn't about to remind her. There was no way to do it without sounding like some cad anyway.

"Did you name the horse?" He chuckled as he banished the thought of her in his arms to the back pastures of his mind.

"No, my fool husband named her. But that was my fault, too. He said she was just as stubborn as me, but he wouldn't curse *her* with *my* name."

An inexplicable rage shot through Conrad's body, and he closed his eyes to rein it in.

"I think you should give her a new name." He turned so

she wouldn't see the anger her words had built. What sort of man needed to cut down his wife like this Lawson? Better that he never find out.

"Perhaps I will, but not today. Today, a new life begins, one where I can finally rest."

He couldn't have stopped himself from turning one last time as she closed her pretty, blue eyes. Izzy Lawson wasn't like any woman he'd ever met, but he still wouldn't let Lula use her to get to him—not even pretty, little Izzy could get him to do something he didn't want to. He'd show them all by staying far from the house, and Izzy. Not even Pa would get him to admit he was a failure and that he couldn't read, not even after years of sitting in a classroom. No pretty bit of a teacher would be able to help him after all this time, either.

CHAPTER 3

I zzy pushed herself up from the couch, her muscles aching. How long had it been since she'd cared about how she felt? The house echoed with the sounds of Lula and her mother-in-law working. Neither of them had been in to look at her in quite a while. She was loath to bother them, but she needed to find relief for nature's ache after drinking so much water when she'd arrived.

Conrad had left out the door at the far end of the room, so that had to be the way out of the house, but where to go from there? Why couldn't she remember getting from the horse to the couch? It was a blur to her. As she pushed open the door, the beauty of the rolling green hills with verdant grass the color of the prettiest emeralds stopped her where she stood. While they were outside of the great Black Hills in Belle Fourche, the land itself seemed to buckle in pretty soft rolls that invited her eyes to roam from one crest to the next.

Barton walked toward her from one of the barns with a ready smile. He had hair the color of caramel and wore every color of brown in both the fabric of his clothes and the dust covering him.

"Afternoon, Izzy. Good to see you again." He tipped his hat to her, ever the gentleman. "Lula came out and told me you'd arrived earlier."

After Barton had been her teacher for a few months at the Normal School, before she'd been married, she couldn't think of him as anything else, not even the husband of her closest friend. Though she'd witnessed the wedding, she hadn't seen them since.

"It's good to see you, as well." She nodded in greeting, but her need was great. Though it was rude, she tipped her head to search around the house.

"I'll show you around, so you know where you can and can't wander, but you're welcome to stay as long as you like. In fact, we'd welcome a nice long visit. Lula doesn't venture to town often, so my ma is her only real companion. I know she's worried with the coming of her time, and who will be here with her."

Though she knew next to nothing about what a birth would entail, that would be a reason to stay. It was so much better than the truth, which was that she wasn't truly welcome anywhere else. She couldn't bear the thought of her mother putting her in mourning. She wasn't mourning and never would, at least, not him. Not in truth.

He first took her around next to the necessary—a whitewashed, functional building far away from the house for privacy—and then, as if he knew her problem without her saying a word, he pointed to the other buildings around, the various barns, the stable, and paddock. He pointed out which fences she had to avoid because of the bulls, and where she should avoid because of steep drop-offs.

As a pair of riders came in, Barton waved and they nodded in return. "On the right is Eli, the left, Arnold. They are the two brothers you haven't met yet, but soon." As she watched the two riders, it was easy to spot how different they were. Eli wasn't as broad of shoulder as Conrad, he was more similar in build to Barton. He had a dark mustache, trimmed nicely, and a gaze that seemed to take in the whole ranch. Arnold wore a red bandanna around his neck that had been over his face. He was dusty from above his nose to his hat.

Barton dipped his hat once again. "I'd best get back to work. Good to see you, Izzy." And he sauntered off, leaving her to her urgent business.

That done, she was able to take a good look around. The front paddock had a stock of fresh horses waiting for the drivers when they returned to exchange a tired mount for a rested one. Beyond that, were two barns, one with machinery and another for calving. They hadn't mattered much when she'd needed the privy, but now that Barton was gone, she could take a closer look. The bull pen was to the left of the machinery barn. Behind the necessary was vast fencing, but none of the cattle were close enough to see.

Izzy roamed to the paddock, unsure of what she should do with her time now that she had neither home, nor husband, to care for. The horses stood about with little to do, in the same predicament as her. The ground was little more than fine dust within the fence, and the horses were saddled, ready for their next rider, but had nothing to do but stand there and swish flies until they were needed. If only she had purpose in the same manner. Even waiting for *something* would be better than knowing nothing. Since she'd wed prior to completing her one year of teacher training, she'd never finished, so she couldn't teach. She had no husband, no future, and no prospects. Before she'd married, Lula had been her only friend.

From the far end of the pasture, a rider approached at a

23

solid lope. His steady form brought to mind home and her own family, all seven of her brothers were cattle ranchers with her father, most of them married. There had been no room left for their one daughter, especially a daughter they'd thought was taken care of. During the two visits her mother had made to see her, she'd tried to impress upon Izzy that sometimes husbands and wives didn't see eye-to-eye. No amount of explaining would dissuade her from that thinking, that what Harland did was more than just *lead* her. To her mother's mind, Izzy's marriage was normal and just fine. To her own, if that was a normal marriage, she never wanted to partake again. Not that anyone was lining up for the job.

The rider drew closer and Izzy backed off from her perch on the bottom rail of the fence. Harland would've said she was too heavy to be standing on it and she might break it. Conrad's handsome face dipped behind the brim of his hat as he nodded and dismounted just outside the corral gate.

"Izzy, good to see you out and about so soon. Wasn't sure if you'd spend the day resting. Seemed like you might need it."

His kind, reassuring words hit her like a brick. Even when Harland had been wooing her, it had been more about stolen kisses than caring words spoken just for her. He'd found out how to reach her parents through the office at the school and had made her ma and pa think things were much more serious between them than they were. He'd come home with her on Christmas holiday and had easily convinced them he was the best man for her. And on the way home, without her parents present, he'd taken her to wed by a judge. She'd been so caught up in the feelings that someone actually wanted her, she hadn't realized important things were missing from their relationship, like the simple care that Conrad had just shown.

"Miss Izzy? Did I say something amiss? I'm sorry." Suddenly, his firm, reassuring hand was on her arm and his face, worry written across his brow, searched her own. How could she have been such a fool to miss those signs in Harland? The clues had been there, and she'd missed them all until it was too late.

"Would you like me to take you back into the house? Maybe being out here is still a little too much. I'm sure Lula has a bonnet you can borrow too, when you're ready."

He didn't move to resume his work, his warm, strong hand lingered on her arm; steady, supportive. He wasn't pushing her or trying to control her. Was she so starved for a kindness that she couldn't even think straight when someone offered her a taste of compassion?

"I-I'm sorry for standing on your fence."

Confusion replaced worry for a moment and he glanced down at her feet.

"Stand on it all you want. I've seen tumbleweeds bigger than you."

She shook her head; his words sounded false to her starved ears. "You're right, I should go back into the house. I'm sorry for bothering you. Please excuse me." She had to get away before she cried in front of this man. He *was* a man, and once she showed a weakness, he would use it against her.

He held her still, and she didn't have the heart to walk away.

"Izzy, you're welcome out here anytime. If you want to ride or go to town, anything, you just let Lula, me, or Barton know. You're our guest and we'll make sure you get whatever you need. You have my word."

She had an overwhelming urge to throw herself into his arms and cry. How could she have been so thoughtless with her life? She'd wanted to be a teacher and it was forbidden that she wed, but she'd done it anyway and ruined her chances of ever teaching anyone. She'd given up her dreams of teaching for a man who didn't love her. Who couldn't even give her the same kindness as this stranger right in front of her.

Conrad's hand slipped off her arm and slid to her back as he drew her along by his side. She'd hardly realized they were moving. When they reached the steps, he slowed his pace so she wouldn't trip over her hems.

"There now. You go rest." He pulled open the door and held it for her. "We'll have you fit as a fiddle before you know it. This land, it heals." His face shone with pride as he turned from her and took in the whole ranch with a sweeping glance, and she couldn't help but follow suit. It was beautiful, the grass greener than she'd ever seen, the sky a perfect blue with wisps of clouds floating on the breeze.

"I pray it does, Conrad."

CONRAD STRODE into his father's den, though his pa had long given up on working the ranch with his sons, they still met there to talk where no hands could hear. His brothers: Arnold, Eli, and Barton, were already waiting for him. They had been through so much together, and even though Barton was a full ten years younger than him, and annoyed him to no end, he'd take a bullet for his little brother.

Arnold glanced up from the conversation and nodded to Conrad. "Now that we're all here, we can get started. Last week, there was some kind of miscommunication and somehow, sacks of flour were ordered instead of grain. We'll never use this much flour and Harvey's won't take it back because they had to order extra just to fill it. We'll have to figure out how to use it."

Conrad had asked Stan to run to the store to pick up the feed he'd ordered the week before, but he'd been sure he'd asked for feed, not flour. What could they do with all that? If he'd gotten the full amount Conrad had asked for, there would be ten, fifty-pound sacks. More than enough for years —if flour would keep—which it wouldn't.

"Are we planning to bake enough bread for the army?" Conrad tried to joke to take the charge out of the room.

He had to get to Stan and talk to him before his brothers did. The problem wasn't funny, but he couldn't have his brothers asking why he hadn't gone to the store himself. He'd only ever gone to pick up orders, not to make them. He didn't even trust himself to take a list that ma or Lula had written, in case Harvey would ask him about something on it. His brothers might not think him fit to stay as majority owner if they knew he couldn't read. He was starting to doubt it himself.

Then again… maybe he could put the new teacher to use. She could read for him. And, if he tried to be smart about it, she might never know it was because he couldn't.

Eli picked at his fingernail, then glanced around the group.

"Don't know about the army, but we might be able to get back a little of that money with a bake sale or something."

Arnold shook his head. "Nope, there's enough flour there to give a bakery a good go. We've got too much to do to be messing with it. Maybe we can see if anyone is in need, but it may just be a loss. We'll store it down in the cellar where it's too cool for the weevils and pray we can find a good use for it."

Conrad stood, ready to be done with the meeting. "Is that all we've got?"

Barton glanced up and a smile slid across his lips. "What is it, big brother? Got plans for the evening? Aren't we good enough company for a few minutes?"

It still irked him that the youngest of the Olesons was the first to marry. *He* should've been first. He should've put more effort into it. Now he was old, having just reached his thirty-first year, too old for the young ladies to look at, and all the more mature women were married, except for Spinster Irma-Jean, but she was a spinster for a reason.

"No, I don't have any plans. I just thought all of you might want to spend an evening in front of the fire instead of together. Since we're with each other all day."

Barton scratched his chin. "I sure do like spending the evening with my wife. Too bad none of you have that option." He laughed as all three brothers flung their hats at him and he dodged out of the line of fire.

Conrad didn't doubt for a second that curling up to something that would curl back was most pleasant, but he'd deal with being alone if that was what the good Lord had planned for him. For now, he had to think of a way to use, or get rid of, that flour. As long as it sat there, the family would wonder about it, and it was only a matter of time before the questions led back to him.

CHAPTER 4

I zzy drew her finger along the spines of the few books in the Oleson family library. There wasn't much to choose from, but that was pretty standard from what she'd seen of rural folk in South Dakota. It wasn't that they didn't put stock in learning, they just tended to spend their money on more practical things. Teachers, scholars, and the philosophical were the exceptions.

Her saddle bag held two of her most treasured books. She'd left the others behind. Perhaps the city would sell those possessions to pay for Harland's burial. In that case, she cared little for what she'd left and prayed the items went to someone who would appreciate them. Either Barton or Lula's teaching primer rested on its back at the end of the shelf, as if it had been referenced since it had been placed. Her own hadn't fit in her hastily packed bag. She'd read the remainder of it, even after she'd married. She'd even read through Harland's homework, and had worked out in her head how she would do each lesson. If she could go back and take the test, she was sure she could pass. But that wasn't meant to be. She had no money for tuition, nor would she feel capable of standing in front of children after the loss of her own.

Her hand absently rubbed at her now empty womb, and she prayed that should she ever find a man who loved her, the Lord wouldn't hold her accountable for Harland's actions. She would have cherished the child, even if it had looked just like him.

Lula swept into the room and Izzy was immediately reminded of the Lula she'd known at school so long ago. Lula had been a breezy spirit, with a ready smile and a big heart. She'd been only fourteen and, at the time, Barton had tormented Lula to get her attention. It hadn't been until he'd come back to the Normal School as her teacher that he'd stopped being a bully and had wooed Lula in a more traditional way, allowing Lula to return to the woman she'd been.

"Are you looking for a little something to occupy your time?" Lula smiled and glanced over Izzy's shoulder at the shelf.

Izzy draped her hands behind her. "I must admit, I feel out of sorts. I haven't been this free with my time since I was a child." The last few months, every moment had been spent attending to Harland. It wasn't until they'd completely run out of food and he was too sick to fight back that he'd let her leave to go to the store. Then he'd accused her of eating them out of house and home. She hadn't had any tears left by then.

Lula rubbed her side gingerly. "I don't think I'll know that feeling again for a long time. This child will be along soon, and then my time will be doubly occupied with chores and caring for the little mite."

That ache struck her own womb once again. "It will be both a joy and a blessing. How long until your time?"

Hopefully it was enough to prepare her own heart for such an occasion.

"The doctor says I have another month. I can't imagine getting much bigger than this." She laughed, but the sound was dry. Even a little frightened.

"Most of your sisters had given birth before you were married. Did you attend any of them?" Izzy had no sisters and, though she'd grown up on a ranch, had never even seen a calf born. Though she was aware of the mechanics of birthing, being a help to a laboring woman would be much more than she was ready for. Terrifying, really, and she was not prepared for her own hurts a birth might bring on.

"No. I was usually one of the girls scuttled out of the house during a birth. Ruby had hers when I was still young. Jennie preferred no one but her husband there. Hattie has never been blessed. Eva and Frances don't live near home, and Nora and Daisy are younger. So, no. I was never able to attend any."

A sick fear plotted a course for Izzy's stomach. She'd faced everything life had thrown at her, but a birth? Why would the Lord make her suffer through watching her closest friend have the one thing she'd been proud of... and lost?

Izzy swallowed her feelings and aimed for a smile. "I'm sure we'll figure it all out once the day arrives. We've got time to plan, and it isn't like Mrs. Oleson hasn't attended one before."

Lula laughed. "Well, she's participated in a few, but I don't know that she's ever been on the other end of the bed. But you're right. We do have plenty of time. I wanted to discuss something with you that is... rather delicate." She turned and strode back across the long room, pulling closed the pocket doors that shut the sitting room off from the rest of the house. The thick oak effectively blocking the noise, silence fell around them.

After already discussing the most delicate subject Izzy could imagine, her thoughts skittered to a stop. "Lula, what's the matter?" Her heart raced. The only time Lula had been secretive with her was when she'd been hiding her relationship with Barton.

"Barton's brother, the one you've met, Conrad, is the matter. I feel you've come to visit us at a most precipitous time, and not just because of this birth." She patted her belly again, but her eyes crinkled with barely-contained concern. "Conrad holds a larger portion of the ranch than any of the other brothers, and we all agree it should stay that way." Lula spun her gold wedding band on her finger as she spoke.

"The problem is that he can't read, and won't admit it. He's taken to trusting men that he shouldn't so he doesn't have to confess his deficit to his brothers. We don't know if the men are turning on Conrad, or if Conrad has lost his love for the ranch, but recently his inability to read cost the ranch more than a month's worth of payroll. So, you see the delicacy in handling this." She tipped her head toward the closed door. "No one must know we spoke about this. Conrad is a proud man and we are not looking to break him, only to help him."

Izzy gasped. She could see, plainly, how Conrad might feel if she knew. He'd also told her, just that day, how he felt the ranch was a place of healing.

"He loves it here. He told me so." It hadn't been in so many words, but his reverence when talking about the healing power of the land had conveyed his love. He wouldn't be a party to destroying anything.

Lula scrunched her lips into a frown. "He's never said as much to me, but something stands between him and me. The relationships here are different than at my home. *My* brothers-in-law on my side of the family all treat me like a sister. Barton's brothers, on the other hand, are cordial, but they don't treat me like family. At least, not yet." A moment of strain passed over Lula's face.

"They may not know how to treat you. They've never had a sister. Give them time. Remember, I come from a large family of brothers, the only girl. Though, I dare say they've treated their own sisters-by-law better than me recently."

Lula led her to the couch and they sat. "I'm so sorry, Izzy."

"You knew. You told me to stop after the first outing with Harland. You told me he was wooing me with promises and little else, and I didn't listen."

Lula took a deep breath and let it out slowly. "I only knew because I saw how he was treating Barton. I heard what he said about you in class after you were married." Lula's cheeks flamed even now, years later.

"You never told me just what he said. Just that he'd spoken of our intimacies in class. I tried so hard to please that man, but nothing I did would measure up. I don't even understand why he wanted me in the first place."

Lula sighed and glanced away, then closed her eyes. "It won't do to dwell on it. As much as it hurts, and it's okay to hurt for a time, you'll never hear an apology from him now, and you can't let him hurt you anymore. But you also can't let him rule you. He's gone, let's keep him that way."

Lula was right. Izzy wouldn't ever receive the kindness from him she'd prayed for. He would never love her now. She was free to move on, but she'd never love again. Love was too vulnerable, and it hurt too badly.

"Now." Lula reached for a small volume on the side table Izzy hadn't noticed. "I need to ask you to do something that

Barton and I have been unable to do. But I think you're just willful enough to handle it."

Izzy straightened her spine. It had been years since anyone had called her that.

"If it's true that Conrad loves this land, then someone is taking advantage of him. The only way to eliminate that advantage... is to take it away." She handed Izzy the small leather-bound book. "You need to teach Conrad to read, and not let him realize you're doing it. He doesn't understand that we know, but it's well-past time. Can you do it?"

Izzy plucked the book from Lula's fingers and ran her hand over the spine. A chance to teach, albeit in secret... Maybe the Lord *was* still listening.

CHAPTER 5

Though it was Sunday, Conrad rarely took the whole day to rest. Cattle didn't rest, so why should he? It wasn't as if they didn't need him. He'd considered just staying home. But Ma expected everyone to ride to service together, piled in one wagon. As he strode to the front yard of his parents' house, it dawned on him. That would mean Izzy would also be riding with them. It had been a tight fit lately, with Lula so ungainly. Now, they would practically be sitting atop one another. His belly tightened a bit. He didn't want Izzy sitting anywhere near his brothers, and certainly not *that* friendly.

Izzy stood near the wagon, eyeing everyone piling in. Her glance slid around and their gazes locked for a moment. There was only one person on that rig he'd let anywhere near his lap, and she was so tiny there was practically room for two of her.

Pa had the draft horses hitched to the wagon and was helping Ma up to her seat. Barton had climbed into the back and held onto both of Lula's hands as she carefully climbed up a few crates to make it to hers. Arnold and Eli followed, leaving him and Izzy the last few inches to squeeze into near the back on each side.

Conrad reached the wagon in time to catch Izzy's worried look at the remaining space. He held out his hand to help her up the crates.

"Don't worry. There will be room for you in the wagon, even if I have to walk or go saddle up quick." She was in the wagon bed by the time he'd finished speaking, and Eli squished closer to Barton to give her room.

"Eli, why don't you move next to Arnold and give her a little space, so our guest doesn't have to dangle off the end of the wagon?"

Eli went red around the ears and stood, giving her his spot and moving next to Arnold. Now Conrad would have a good excuse to sit next to her. He hopped up the crates and into the back, settling himself next to Izzy. There wasn't much room. One good bump and his Sunday best would hit the gravel. He draped his arm behind Izzy and gripped the side of the wagon. She didn't protest, but she also went rigid as an oak tree to keep from touching him. Her face held so much sadness, but he knew if he could catch happiness there, she would be far more beautiful than any woman he'd ever laid eyes on.

Her voice was barely above a whisper as she tilted her chin down toward him, taking him into confidence.

"Would you walk with me later, show me around the ranch a little?" She colored just a bit. "You did say if I needed anything, I should but ask…"

He *had* said that. And he would do his darnedest not to let it go to his head she was asking him and not Barton or Lula, whom she knew.

"When we get back from the church picnic." He nodded.

"Or will you be too tired?" She'd looked so peaked when he'd found her the day before.

Lula cleared her throat, drawing his attention.

"Eli and Arnold, I'd like to introduce you to my closest and most dear friend, Izzy Lawson. She'll be staying with us until she tires of our company, so do your best not to wear her out too quickly. I'd like to keep her around a good long while."

Barton squeezed his wife closer to his side. Though he worked hard all day—he was, after all, an Oleson—he was distracted. Barton wanted to be with his wife every minute he wasn't working, often leaving chores early or delegating them to the hands. Her burgeoning size had only made it worse.

Conrad leaned closer to Izzy. "We don't have to go today if it will tire you."

She laughed. The first he'd heard from her. "I wouldn't have asked you if I thought I wouldn't be able."

He nodded, too pleased to trust his own throat with the words. The sermon would seem even longer than usual today.

Four hours later, Conrad waited in the sitting room for Izzy to come down. She'd helped Lula up the stairs to lie down after the service and the picnic. Izzy had sat next to him during the luncheon affair, eating less than a bird and nervous about every bite. She seemed to hide the fact she was eating at all and, finally, he'd just gotten up to give her some space. He prayed she'd take a few bites once he left. There had been little to talk about anyway, and now he worried their walk would seem just as strained.

Izzy softly padded down the long staircase in her slippers and stopped at the landing. "I'm sorry that took so long. Lula was quite uncomfortable, and it took me longer than expected to help her. It appears I'm not well-suited to helping women in pain."

Since she wouldn't jump to her own defense, he needed to. "I don't think it has to do with you. I remember when Ma was going to have Barton, there wasn't anything that could make her comfortable near the end. She just toiled anyway. With three older boys, she couldn't take a break, and she never did get the help she was hoping for with a girl."

Izzy's eyes flashed for just a moment, then she tipped her head, hiding her face. "I should say she did. She has a daughter now that Lula is here."

He hadn't really thought of Lula as a sister—a pretty distraction for his brother—but not a sister. "Where would you like to explore?"

Izzy tilted her chin down and closed her eyes. He'd never just let himself talk with a woman like this, and watching every expression cross her face was like an explorer forging new territory. She was a beautiful, uncharted land to explore, and he loved every quirk of her pretty lips and dazzling eyes.

"I think I'd like to see the pastures. The hills are so pretty and nothing like what I'm used to. Maretta packed a supper for us in case we're out too late."

He'd never heard anyone call his mother Maretta, and though he knew her name, it sounded so strange on Izzy's lips. "Ma packed a picnic?" He wouldn't complain, but two meals on the grass in one day was a little too much like traveling, something he never got to do and didn't really wish to.

Her lip disappeared between her teeth for a moment. "If you'd rather not, I can just leave it. I'm sure I don't need any supper anyway."

Land sakes, why would she think he was trying to take away her meal? She could eat twice what was in that basket and she'd still need to eat more to put a little meat on her bones.

"I wasn't thinking anything of the sort. I just wasn't sure you wanted to be out long enough to need it. If you want me to keep you out that long, I'm sure I can manage." He tried to sound warm, welcoming. Talking to Izzy was like waltzing with a partner who only knew how to two-step, and he seemed to step on her feet often without trying.

She turned and he followed her to the kitchen. While it was the women's domain, he'd grown up in that house and it seemed as natural as breathing to follow her. She slid to a stop and angled her head back toward him in front of the door.

Her eyes darted from his chest up to his face and her mouth hung open slightly as her eyes widened. He backed away a step to give her room, those amazing blue eyes still stared at him, with far too much fear than he ever wanted to see there. An urge to pull her close and protect her from whatever ghost haunted her slipped over him like a mantle.

"I'm just going to get the basket. I'll be right back. You don't have to follow…"

He didn't feel like just waiting for her. He'd waited the whole time she'd been helping Lula and he was antsy to go. "It's no matter. I can get the basket and we can go out the kitchen door."

Izzy hesitated for a moment, then pushed forward into the room just out of his reach. He followed her, grabbed the basket, and waited for her to put her bonnet on and tie it. As she tucked the wisps of hair by her face back under the fabric, he wanted to tell her just how pretty she was, but it wasn't his place to do so. Her hair was a gentle brown with just enough thickness to it that a man could lose his hands in it. Her nose upturned just a bit at the end, giving her a look of alertness to go with her blue eyes.

Descending the back porch, they stepped out into the afternoon sun. His brothers would pick up the slack on this rare day that he wouldn't be working, and he refused to feel guilty about it. They had all done extra chores when Barton was at school for three years and had thought he wasn't coming back. Now, Barton could shoulder a little more for an afternoon. Also, it would make up for the days he wouldn't work once his son or daughter was born. Conrad would work extra time to make sure Barton could spend time with the new babe.

The pasture was so huge that none of the cattle were within sight. He lifted the metal c-ring holding the gate closed and let Izzy in, then followed, locking the gate behind them. While a pasture seemed an unlikely place for a stroll, he wouldn't complain. Izzy wandered toward a small copse of trees and he followed her natural curiosity. That spot would make a nice place to sit for a while if she wanted to, once they reached it.

Her shoulders were set and she seemed to want to talk to him about something, though he couldn't imagine what. They had no history. Unless she'd figured out it had been him who'd carried her into the house and she was embarrassed, but then why would she be out alone with him? Worry crept over him. If Izzy really had been asked by her friend to come teach him to read, as he suspected, he'd have to guard his words. Could she have asked him out here to corner him into admitting his failure?

He lengthened his stride to catch up to her. "I've got to say, while I don't mind a bit taking you out here, the pasture is one place you're probably safe to explore on your own. A child might not be, but a woman full-grown has the sense to stay away from the cows. You seem like a woman who's got plenty of sense." He kept watch on his feet, worried his words, as they so often seemed to, would bother her yet again. It wasn't until he'd almost passed her that he realized she'd stopped.

"I *could* explore on my own, but I was hoping to go farther than just these little trees. It certainly doesn't *seem* as if you don't mind taking me. If being here with me has taken you away from something important, then by all means…" Her shoulders slumped and she turned back for the house, but her feet didn't move.

He was too big to worry about walking on eggshells. They'd all crack anyway. "Miss Izzy, I don't know what makes you so sensitive to everything I say, but you shouldn't be. I haven't once thought poorly of you. In fact, I've had some rather nice thoughts of you." He took a step closer to her. "Like when you 'bout passed clean out into my arms as you fell off your horse and I carried you into the house. That was probably the most pleasant thing that's ever happened to me. Best luck I've ever had."

Izzy gasped and clutched her thin arms tightly about her middle. "I'm so sorry." She spun from him, but not before her face turned a beautiful shade of pink. "That must have been dreadful."

Infernal woman! Deaf as a stump. "Blast, woman! Didn't you hear a word I just said? It wasn't dreadful in the slightest. I'd do it again in a heartbeat. Want a go?" He took a step closer to her, only half joking. He *would* pick her up again and hold her close, but only if she'd let him.

She swung to face him, her eyes wide, her hand flattened against his chest and he stopped immediately. "Conrad. You don't understand." Her beautiful lips parted as she sighed and backed away from him once again. "My husband told me the truth, what you see isn't. I'm not..." Her words died as she searched his face, but he couldn't help her. He couldn't find a fault with her.

"I don't know what you mean, Izzy. I *carried* you. It wasn't about *seeing* anything except a woman who was going to fall in the dirt, and I wasn't about to let that happen."

She huffed and gathered herself up straight. Somewhere inside that woman was a strong backbone that had been worn thin as a wheat stalk. But could she get back her pluck?

"Let's go sit down under the trees for a minute. I need a rest." She turned and strode quickly away. Much too quickly for a woman in need of a *rest*.

CHAPTER 6

There was too much debris under the trees to lay the blanket, and Izzy didn't want to take the time to clean it. Conrad would be there in a thrice and he'd want to know why she'd run off when they were talking. She couldn't come right out and say how terrified she was of being *big*. How many times had Harland told her she was *too big*? It didn't matter that Conrad had carried her, held her in his arms, he was also one of the most muscled men she'd ever seen. *Of course* she seemed light to him; she could weigh as much as horse and he'd probably think her like a feather. But she wasn't. What Harland said was fact, it always was. No questions asked.

Conrad set the basket down and rested his hands on his lean hips. He was so much better formed than Harland had ever been. She'd thought Harland bookish, but handsome. Conrad was work-hewn, sturdy, with a pleasant mustache that was trimmed well, and a firm jawline. His shoulders were wide and he stood at least a full head taller than her. Strange how frightening the smaller man seemed to her. Conrad could crush her in a moment, but he wouldn't.

43

Harland couldn't hurt a fly, yet he'd killed her in other ways. Conrad took off his hat and tossed it atop the basket, revealing the same caramel hair as Barton, and just as neat.

She drew closer to pull the blanket out of the basket. Conrad stood next to it, his feet planted apart, watching her with a million unasked questions on his face. Izzy took a deep breath and reached for the basket when her knees buckled right out from under her and she screeched, clutching for whatever she could and coming up with a fistful of Conrad's shirt.

The jawline she'd been admiring just a moment before was now only a few inches away as he gave her a smug look.

"See, you're no bigger than an ant. Point of fact, I'm hoping Ma packed extra in that basket. It gets powerful windy here, I'd like to see you make it through a stiff wind or two."

Izzy's heart rattled against her chest and still he didn't put her down. The insufferable man seemed quite pleased at making his point. "Are you finished, Mr. Oleson?" she hissed. "Put me down!"

His dark brown eyes burned into her own, the specks of gold burning bright within. Heat sprang to life inside her, and she couldn't tear her gaze from his.

"I'd rather not. You can't run away from me up here." He laughed as he set her back down on her feet just as easily as he'd scooped her up. Though her legs were now wobblier than they'd been a moment before, and she held tight to his shirt for a minute longer. His hands held her elbows as her gaze slid first to his soft-looking lip under his mustache, then up to those beautiful eyes.

"I'm so sorry." She yanked her hands back into fists to keep from touching him again. The creases in his shirt would need to be pressed out.

Her skirts felt as out of sorts as she was. She smoothed and swished them to get them to settle just right as Conrad bent and flipped open the lid of the basket, retrieving the blanket. Her intimate behavior hadn't seemed to ruffle *him* a bit, only his shirt front. He spotted the place with the least twigs and flicked the blanket, letting it settle easily over the grass.

Finding a way to get Conrad to read without letting him in on the secret would be difficult with him interrupting her thoughts at each turn. He may be completely ashamed his family let her in on such a secret. Her stomach roiled at the tension, and she wasn't yet ready to eat. It was too early and her insides were in a terrible tizzy over what he'd just done, and what *she'd* just done. Why did men always have to prove they were right?

Conrad moved the basket to the edge of the blanket, then lowered himself next to where she stood. He stared up at her with eyes that had cooled to liquid chocolate. Her traitorous belly did another jig. If she hurt this man's pride, he may never want anything more to do with her, and at this moment, he was the only man she would allow in her life, even Barton would remain at arm's length. Was it worth the risk?

"Are you going to sit? I thought you needed a rest?" One side of his mouth quirked into a smile. Yes, he was an insufferable man. And he'd seen right through her.

Izzy picked a spot on the blanket on the opposite corner from him and peered into the basket, unsure of herself and what she should say or do. Teaching had drawn her like a moth to flame, but now that she'd lost the right to call herself a teacher, every doubt erupted into her thoughts to combat her. Teaching Conrad to read was the right thing to do, but was she the right teacher for the job? She drew a small book from the basket, one of the few precious books she'd brought with her, and she clutched it to her chest for strength. *Lord, help me do right by this man.*

The smile died on Conrad's lips and fear slid up and choked her words.

"What do you have there?"

Izzy took a deep breath. "It's my favorite book of poetry. I was hoping you'd let me read you a few... But, maybe that was just silly. I'll put it away." She raised up onto her knees to open the basket, but Conrad caught her wrist gently. His grip was nothing like Harland's. Though his touch was soft, and she could've easily shaken him off, she didn't want to. He sent pleasant waves like a current into her, and the longer he held her, the more pleasant they became.

"I don't mind. If that's the way you like your poetry, go ahead and read it. I've never liked fancy words much, myself." His voice was too quiet, too reserved. She'd hit him where he hurt and he was trying to cover it up.

Why had she thought he might enjoy poetry? She'd packed the book hoping the short nature of poems would help his interest. "My particular favorite doesn't really have pretty words." She opened to the first page and took a deep breath. Praying something would touch him and let her in, give her some way to help him.

"Was it for this that one, the fairest of all rivers,
loved to blend his murmurs with my Nurse's song,
And from his alder shades, and rocky falls,
And from his fords and shallows, sent a voice
That flowed along my dreams?"

She sighed and slid back against the tree. "I used to dream that Harland would read to me. But he never did." Why did thoughts of that goat have to ruin her time with Conrad? But he was still a part of her, gone but still hovering over her like a fomenting cloud. She couldn't rid herself of him.

Conrad didn't look up at her. "There were many things he didn't do for you, or so it would seem." Conrad leaned back on his elbow, his jawline hard.

"That may be, and perhaps not all women feel this way, but this one wishes she'd married the romantic man she thought she was getting."

He laid back and cradled his head with his interwoven hands. "There's more to life than a man repeating someone else's words. What about a man's *own* words, aren't they important? Romance isn't worth much if it's false, if the feelings aren't there and it's just rote."

Izzy sighed and closed the book. He was right. And what he'd just said was more sweet and romantic than Harland had ever managed. Even if Harland *had* read her hours of poetry, it wouldn't make up for all the other things he'd done. The only words he'd spoken from his heart had torn her to shreds. But right now, it was Conrad's truth that left her feeling open, raw, and wounded. Not only that, she was already pushing Conrad away with her clumsy attempts, and she hadn't even figured out how to teach him yet.

The best teacher in the world wasn't a person, it was motivation. And once again, she'd assumed that since he'd wanted to spend time with *her*, she could gain his interest by using her feminine wiles to motivate him. She should've known better. Hadn't Harland taught her she was worse than a toad, that she wasn't worthy of being desired? No man would ever consider her a motivation to do anything, except perhaps run.

"Of course they are. I just enjoy *this* man's words." She dropped the book to her lap and fought against the burn of tears behind her eyes.

Conrad sat up, all the warmth gone from his face. "Well, perhaps you can get him to read them to you." Conrad's tone was rough, unyielding. She backed away from him further on the blanket and slipped the book back into the basket. She turned from him, pushing to her feet.

"I don't think he's available. He died over fifty years ago." Her heart ached for love, not the love she'd never had from Harland, she couldn't miss what was foreign to her. He'd robbed her of the love of her closest friend, and her family as well, and she couldn't face Conrad and his harsh truth. Not without spilling all her empty, craving heart out to him. She would never be ready for that. Izzy strode further, deeper into the small copse of trees and away from Conrad, away from admitting her faults and fears. It wouldn't matter anyway. She couldn't teach him, shouldn't have even tried. She was no teacher, she was nothing.

When she returned, he'd gathered the blanket and it was back in the basket. He sat, leaned up against the tree with his hat hiding his face. He flipped it up and glanced up at her. It hadn't been long, but she wouldn't ask him to stay out any longer and waste more of his time.

"I hope you found the peace you were looking for, and I hope you find someone to read to you, Izzy. You deserve someone who'll give you everything you desire, and more." His quiet voice thrummed through her. How could she let this handsome man get to her so? She hadn't been a widow half as long as she should've been before even looking to another man. But she'd never been a true, cherished wife, either. He lifted the basket as he stood, then waited for her.

"I don't think there will be much finding, Conrad. I'll just settle for reading to myself." The hurt was easy to hide, she'd done it for a year and a half. She swung past him and headed back for the house.

"Both of my brothers can read." His voice was so quiet, so full of an ache she'd never heard the likes of before. Those words had eaten his pride just to pass his lips.

She wouldn't make him admit anything. That hadn't been her goal. She'd wanted to build him up, to make him realize he was a worthy man so that when she did try to teach him, he would know she didn't think him any less of a man. She'd done just the opposite.

"I've heard Barton read a blackboard full of notes, and he does bore one to tears. I wouldn't ever ask him to read Wordsworth to me."

Her attempt at humor missed the target completely. "My other brothers can read, too." Why was he admitting his faults to her when he hadn't been willing to tell his own family? Why did he trust her with his secret?

Izzy stopped and turned to look him in the eye, her need to make amends for the damage she'd wrought was so great.

Izzy closed her eyes and prayed the Lord would take away her fear of speaking, and more, that her words would hit their mark. "I wouldn't ask your brothers to read to me. But, I'd ask you."

0KVOGF00CW1J

Title	TEACH ME TO LOVE (BROTHERS OF BE
Condition	Good
Location	Walden Aisle Z Bay 42 Item 6248
Description	May have some shelf-wear due to normal use. Your purchase funds free job training and education in the greater Seattle area. Thank you for supporting Goodwill's nonprofit mission!
Source	Prescanned
SKU	0KVOGF00CW1J
ASIN	1717404898
Code	9781717404893
Employee	1dfields
Date Added	1/5/2024 10:06:55 AM

CHAPTER 7

A man shouldn't have to have words sound through his head all day. Conrad kept telling himself not to dwell on Izzy's challenge from the day before. There were thousands of men in South Dakota, and out of all of them, she'd chosen him. *Him.* To *read.* Maybe a lot of them couldn't, but, at the moment, he sure felt like the only one with such a failing.

After he'd made it back to his home that evening and laid on his lonely bed, he'd done little else but think about her words. *I wouldn't ask your brothers to read to me. But, I'd ask you.*

Now, after a long day in the saddle staying far away from his parents' house and Izzy Lawson, he was no closer to convincing his thoughts to leave off. He'd also done something that he now regretted...

Conrad pushed himself off his bed and slid his hand under his pillow, retrieving the book Izzy had read from. He'd looked through the first few pages, but couldn't make hide nor hair out of the lines on the page. He knew his letters, but the sounds each one made had always been a mystery. The longer the word, the more his head just wouldn't work when faced with the problem of translating the symbols to sounds.

Izzy hadn't given him the challenge, yet when he'd taken the volume, he'd tucked it into his vest on the way back to the house. Now he wanted to try... for her. That's why he'd taken it. He had no books in his whole house. The way Izzy had held the book close to her meant she probably loved it, and she had probably already missed it. She would know he'd taken it, so it was best to get the embarrassment over and return it to her, since he couldn't read it anyway.

He shoved himself from his bed, donning his hat along the way, and strode out into the twilight. If she wasn't awake, he'd just leave the book in the sitting room and she'd find it in the morning. If she was awake... he'd have to confess to taking it. If he didn't come up with a good reason, she might ask him if he enjoyed the poems. Then she'd want to know if he'd found a favorite. That was what intelligent people did. They discussed poetry and talked a lot. He'd never been welcome in those circles and had never cared about the lack until just then, and it made him pert-near sick thinking about it. Izzy was an intelligent woman, could've been a teacher. And he was just a rancher. Worse, a rancher who couldn't even read.

He had no business even looking at her, but he couldn't stop thinking about her, much less stop his gaze from fixing on her whenever she was nearby. Or picturing the soft curve of her lips, the taper of her neck, her narrow waist... He shook his head. His *not* thinking about her was leading him down trails that would get him into trouble.

He stopped at the edge of the porch bathed in the slight glow of the lamplight from the sitting room window. Inside, Izzy sat on the sofa with her head bent, concentrating on something. Her forehead was wrinkled slightly and her eyes were narrowed. Though he wanted to give the book back to her, he also didn't want to disturb whatever she was doing.

The door swung open and Barton waved as he let the door shut behind him. "Evening, Conrad. Nice night for a walk. Thought I'd do the same."

Barton never seemed to do anything without Lula, yet here he was, interrupting a perfect night.

"Will your wife be joining you?"

He stopped for a moment. "No, she's too tired. Too close to her time."

"I wasn't quite sure you could still breathe without her approval." Taunting Barton was just too much of a temptation; something drove him, and he wanted Barton as grumpy as he was.

"Not tonight, brother." Barton wouldn't rise to the barb. He glanced just behind his shoulder through the window. "Maybe chatting with a frustrated female will soothe the savage beast." He tipped his head and sauntered off into the night.

Conrad couldn't keep his gaze from wandering to the window, and Izzy ducked her head quickly to escape being seen watching him. She had to have heard; her cheeks went pink in the soft golden glow of the lamp. The glass was too thin to stop the noise of their conversation. She would've heard his baited comments. That drained all the fight out of him. His thoughtless words would make her think he was rude.

No sense turning back now, she'd seen him standing there and that he hadn't followed Barton. The distance to the door seemed a mile long as he trudged up the stairs and pulled the door wide. As he stepped inside, Izzy glanced up from her book as if she'd just discovered he was there. He had to hold in a laugh, she was a terrible actress, and that pleased him. If she couldn't act, she couldn't lie.

"Good evening, Conrad. I was sorry you didn't join us for supper tonight." The play of the light on her pale skin was a glorious sight, distracting him for a moment too long.

He'd thought about joining them, but his parents would've thought it strange, and so would Barton. They might wait until a private moment, but they would rib him about spending time with Mrs. Lawson. His ma wouldn't have it if she knew he'd thought about her more than he ought. Izzy was a widow who should be in mourning, not out taking strolls with him.

"Evening." He realized she was still waiting for his greeting. "I don't usually eat up here. Not really my place."

She stood and clasped her tiny hands in front of her, her pretty, softly arched lips quivering slightly. "Barton and his wife were here. It was a pleasant meal. I hope you'll come once in a while."

Why wasn't she asking about either of his other two brothers? Was it only him she wanted to see, or was he inspecting her words too closely?

"I guess if Ma wants me to come, she'll extend an invitation."

Izzy nodded and turned from him. "We spoke at supper about some excess flour sitting in the cellar. Maretta said that I might speak to you about using it?" She glanced over her shoulder at him, pale as a sheet. Why would she be so nervous about talking to him... unless his family had told her it was his fault they had so much flour.

"Why ask me about it?" He took a deep breath to keep the edge from his voice. No sense in scaring her yet again. At least she was talking to him.

"Maretta said you might have plans for it, and that I

should speak to you. She just wasn't sure if it had a purpose and didn't want me to make plans and then be disappointed."

He didn't want her to be disappointed, either. "What did you have in mind?"

She turned back to him and a fresh glow lit her face, which would've shocked him if he hadn't imagined just that look on her face all day long.

"It's wonderful, really. Maretta said there's a storefront in town that used to be a boarding house. It has two large baking ovens in the back. I was thinking of staying in Belle Fourche and starting a bakery." She searched his face, her own open with excitement.

Baking wasn't the first thing he thought of when he saw her. "Are you sure? That's what you want to do?"

The happiness slipped off her like snow off a roof, and he could've kicked himself. He'd done it yet again. When would he learn to keep his mouth shut?

"I guess it's a rather silly idea. Think nothing of it." Tension coiled in her words, hurt long buried.

"I didn't say it was a silly idea, I just asked if you were sure. Taking on a new business is a big responsibility, and you just got here. You were so weak you couldn't even make it in the house. Not to mention, you wouldn't be out here much if you were working in town." And maybe that bothered him most of all. "Didn't Lula want you out here with her?" If he gave what should be her reason for staying, she may never suspect any other.

She wouldn't raise her head, it stayed bent like a reed in the wind.

"There's nothing for me out here, Conrad. I grew up on a ranch, but there's nothing I can do to help. I need to find some reason to get up in the morning. I'm not doing anyone any good. Lula needs a friend, but I don't want to stay underfoot. Your ma certainly doesn't need me around. She's the most ingenious woman I've ever met."

He chuckled, despite Izzy's words. "That she is, but I still don't want to see you run off into town and start a business just because there are a few sacks of extra flour laying around. I'm sure there's plenty to do here, if you really wanted to put yourself to it. You haven't come near to wearing out your welcome yet." He handed her the book. The whole reason he'd ventured from home and he'd almost forgotten it.

She stared first at the book, then up at him. "You had it? I thought I'd left it by the tree and I was worried it had been ruined outside. But... why? You said you don't like poetry."

That was the most difficult question she could ask as she searched his eyes for the truth before he could even speak. "I just wanted to look at it. I should've asked. I'm sorry for taking your book. I came back here tonight to return it."

She picked the volume from his fingertips and set it on the table. "Oh. Well, I guess since you've done what you came to do..." She sat back down on the couch and laid her hands in her lap.

Did she have to look so forlorn? So completely lonely? Like him? And why did he feel the need to fix it? It shouldn't matter to him one bit if she were lonely. She was Lula's guest, not his.

"I did have a question for you." He breathed deeply. Why wasn't this easy? "I have some trouble understanding... poetry. Would you read it with me, help me understand what he's talking about?"

There. He hadn't admitted he couldn't do what most seven-year-olds could. Most men his age wouldn't know the first thing about poetry.

Her face lit back up, the glow slamming into his chest and

warming him from the inside out. She was gorgeous when she smiled.

"Of course! I'd love to." She stood and grasped his hand with more strength than he'd given her credit for and dragged him to the sofa, which he wouldn't have minded in the slightest if it had been for anything but reading. Before he could protest, she shoved him down into the seat and sat next to him, the scent of her hair breezing past his nose.

"Perfect. We'll start with Wordsworth."

Conrad bit his tongue. He'd gotten himself into a mess of hot water now.

CHAPTER 8

I t hadn't quite been an invitation to teach him to read, but it was as close as she might ever get. Izzy had promised Lula she'd try to get through to Conrad, but she'd been unsure of just how. Now she knew. Wordsworth. Most of the words were simple. If she'd tried to get out a beginning primer, he'd have known her purpose and would have been embarrassed by her prodding.

She avoided looking at him, so he wouldn't see how she worried over each word. "Poetry is a little different than usual books. It's more about conveying a feeling than it is about story, usually. Poets are highly skilled and pick just the perfect words with the exact meaning they are looking for. They don't always rhyme, but some do."

"This guy didn't rhyme." Conrad pointed to the book.

She couldn't help but notice his glance flitting to the door, or his hands clasped tightly in his lap. He wanted to be anywhere but there with her. While Wordsworth was not all that difficult to understand, perhaps simpler poetry would be better, and a more lyrical poem might be easier to read. She stood and searched the shelf for a book that had been there the day before. One with simple lines and couplet form.

"Why don't we plan to do this another day? It's getting a mite late and I've got to be up with the sun tomorrow." Conrad stood, his bent shoulders reminding her of a boy caught being naughty. Would he ever believe that she didn't think less of him? That she was tired of the scholarly, and wanted nothing to do with a man who put the love of learning and books above his love of her.

Izzy went to meet him as he paused at the door. "I'm glad you came by. Thank you for returning my book. I'm so glad it wasn't ruined. But anytime you want to borrow it, you may. I trust you."

He gazed down into her eyes. So tall above her yet she felt so protected near him.

"Why? You have no reason to."

But deep down, she did. The man was honesty, safety, strength, and security, all in a rather appealing package.

"But I do. I've seen what untrustworthy men look like. I know how they speak in sweet tones around others and turn viper as soon as a door closes. I know how they steal kisses and convince their prey they are good. You don't do that. You, I trust."

His head dipped just slightly and his gaze flitted to her lips. "Don't put me on a pedestal. Any man worth his salt would try to steal a kiss from a pretty lady."

His words released a stampede of feelings inside her that she was unprepared to handle. When she'd first met Harland, his kiss had been nice. Almost addicting. Certainly exciting because it was forbidden. But after their wedding night, everything had changed. She'd still wanted him with the passion she'd known nothing about, but he wanted nothing to do with her. She'd let him down, and if she wasn't careful, she could do that to Conrad, too. There was no cure for a loveless, passionless marriage, and she wouldn't do that to Conrad.

"You haven't tried yet, and we've been alone twice. I'd say that means either you're trustworthy or—"

His face hardened and he shoved his hat on his head, hiding his eyes from her. "You're beautiful, and if you don't believe me, I'll show you." He stepped toward her.

Izzy backed away. She hadn't thought for a moment he would disagree with her, but shouldn't she have expected it? Hadn't he aimed to prove how right he was just the day before in the pasture when he'd swept her right off her feet?

He flinched at her reaction and shook his head as he turned for the door. "I don't want to hear any more nonsense. Next time you want to spout such hogwash, I won't threaten, I'll just prove you wrong." The door slammed shut and she jumped at the sharp noise.

She covered her lips with her fingers as she watched Conrad walk through the fading lamplight and into the darkness. Only a year and a half separated her from her first kiss, but her lips had only touched Harland's. Would Conrad be different? Would his lips bring that excitement, or would she be so terrified of disappointing him that she wouldn't feel a thing?

Izzy picked up the paper she'd been writing on before he'd come in. She'd been trying to remember her mother's recipe for sweet rolls. Something was missing and the only way to figure it out was a day in the kitchen. Lula and Maretta would love to help her. At least it would keep her busy and not thinking about kissing lips that were covered with a handsomely trimmed mustache.

CHAPTER 9

The dough looked just as Izzy remembered, and the smell was heavenly. It had been so long since she'd baked anything, and if her mama were there, she'd be elated. Izzy stopped her stirring in the midst of the massive kitchen. Except, her mama *wouldn't* be happy, because her mama had no idea where she was. She probably didn't even know about Harland's death.

Lula stopped her chatting and laid a hand on Izzy's arm. "Is everything all right? Those rolls smell wonderful, but I'm worried. If it takes this long to bake one batch you'll never have time to sleep! It takes a lot of work to run a bakery. Are you sure this is what you want to do?"

Izzy stepped back from the dough and took in the messy kitchen. The rolls did take a long time between the rising and the rolling, but what else could she do well? Cooking had always been a talent, one she hadn't been able to use since Harland had been so disagreeable. If she didn't start the bakery, she'd have to go home eventually, and she'd rather pluck every hair out of her head one by one than go home.

Conrad strode in the back door and took a deep sniff.

The moment he entered the kitchen, she felt his presence and she reached for her hair, realizing too late that she'd probably just floured her head. He strode farther into the room, his eyes dancing.

"My, that wonderful smell drew me in from a hundred yards away and through both the patio and the back door."

Maretta smiled at her oldest son. "Izzy's testing out some recipes to see if she has what it takes to run a bakery."

She hadn't gotten approval from Conrad the night before, but she *would* repay him for the flour. A bakery was something she could do, something worthwhile. But her doubt continued to whisper in her ears. Harland would certainly say she had no business running a bakery. She forced herself to look up at Conrad. He'd been nothing like Harland. He'd never taken advantage of her when they were alone or made her feel like the grass on the bottom of his boot.

"I don't expect you to just give me your supplies, Conrad. I'll repay everything." If she did, no one could hold anything over her head, she wouldn't be beholden to anyone.

"The money is spent and would've gone to waste otherwise. And it isn't like I won't benefit from your baking." He ran his finger along the top of the cinnamon glaze bowl and slowly plunged it between his lips, closing his eyes. Her heart leapt to life as she watched him. How could something so innocent make her feel so wobbly?

"That's right fine," he said, his approval sent her spirit soaring.

As he opened his eyes, his gaze landed on her and he smiled, making her wonder if he meant the glaze... or her. He'd given her just what she'd wanted; she'd aimed to please him.

"Thank you. I've got a few other things to try. I hope

you'll come for supper tonight. We'll be tasting everything after."

Maretta piped up. "Yes, tell Eli and Arnold, too. We want as many people to try them as possible." Nathan, Conrad's father, slid in behind Maretta and stole one of the finished rolls that had just cooled enough to eat. Maretta swatted his hand, but too late, the confection was gone in one big bite.

"That is, if there's any left by tonight." Maretta laughed as she squeezed Nathan's hand. He swiped it, lifting her arm high and turning her easily in a waltz only the two of them could hear.

Distracted by Conrad's parents, Izzy startled when he brushed her ear with a kitchen towel. He'd somehow managed to get just behind her and leaned in, his voice vibrated through her in a low whisper. "Are you sure you want to do this? You don't have to go."

That moment, she didn't want to go anywhere. He was so near she couldn't think properly, and his family was so close to what she'd always desired; welcoming, loving.

"I don't want to go, but I can't stay where I'm not useful."

He glanced to the others in the room, then took her arm and led her out of the kitchen. When they reached the hall, he stopped. The space was narrow and he took up most of it. She flattened herself against the wall to keep from touching him.

"What about teaching me poetry. That's something."

She couldn't argue that, but he didn't want to learn from her, if all his shifting and excuses last night were any indication.

"I know poetry doesn't really interest you, Conrad. You don't have to pretend to like it so that I'll think more highly of you." She looked him in the eye to get her point across because it was so important he believe her. "I already do."

Conrad took a deep breath. "What if I want you to do it for other reasons?"

He wouldn't meet her eyes. She wouldn't push him to learn to read, but she'd only do it if he really wanted to. Spending the time with him would be far too pleasant to say no.

"There are things... I don't understand, but I want to. I'm tired of relying on everyone else when I shouldn't have to. Will you help me, Izzy?" His plea broke her heart. No one had ever trusted her so completely. How could she possibly say no when she wanted to say yes so badly?

She reached out and touched his muscled arm, so hard beneath her fingers. "I'll help you, Conrad. I promise. Then, when you've learned all you can from me. Will you help me?" Her words were small, though she ached to be strong.

"Help me to start over. Help me to start the bakery or find something I can do to be useful. I don't want to be worthless anymore." The strength to admit what she needed had come from somewhere within. She hadn't even realized what she was saying until it was out of her mouth.

Conrad leaned forward and braced both of his hands on either side of her shoulders, trapping her in place, not that she wanted to leave. Her breath caught in her throat, remembering his words from the night before. *Next time you want to spout such hogwash, I won't threaten, I'll just prove you wrong.* But would he? She made the mistake of letting her gaze fall to his lips then back to his eyes as they widened in surprise. He leaned forward and the heat from him penetrated through all her layers and deep into her.

"You aren't worthless, but I suspect the one who told you such is... Or should I say... was?" He waited for her to answer, but she couldn't.

Even now, saying anything aloud about Harland left her

sick to her stomach with fear. Conrad raised a hand and lifted her chin. She held her breath, hoping, wondering...

"That man wasn't worth the air the Good Lord let him breathe. He lied to you, Izzy." Conrad pushed away from the wall and apart from her. He wasn't going to kiss her, and she felt cold, exposed, and raw without his nearness.

"So, you won't help me, then." She slid along the wall back toward the kitchen, the bitter taste of rejection a familiar companion.

"I'll help you find what you want to do, Isabelle, but you've got to find your worth yourself. I can't give that to you." He'd called her *Isabelle*...

He turned and strode out the front door, but he could've just as well stayed. His words cascaded around inside her and the more they rang in her head, the angrier she got. Harland had taken more from her than she ever should've let him. But he wouldn't take any more. And if Conrad was there to help her, she could heal and be the woman she was before Harland's poison began seeping into her blood. Izzy stood tall and shoved her way back into the kitchen, so thankful for a big strong man who threatened to kiss her, but didn't have to in order to get his point across.

CHAPTER 10

His mood vacillated from an aching desire to stride right back into his parents' house and show Isabelle just how pretty and worthy she was, to wanting to find some way to avenge her feelings after she'd been married to that good-for-nothing... *teacher*.

Oh, *Isabelle*. The name fit her so much better than Izzy. She was a beautiful woman, not some child. And he'd let it slip in his weakness. He couldn't think of her as Izzy. She was Isabelle, a beautiful, captivating woman.

He clenched his fist and strode into the barn. Stan stood against the back wall, waiting for him. His hat tilted at an angle that hid his eyes, the only thing visible was the smirk on his lips.

"I got the hands, like you said. Twenty-five of them."

Twenty-five? He'd asked for five. "I know I only asked you for five men, Stan."

The wrangler flicked his toothpick from one side of his mouth to the other. "Nope, I distinctly remember you saying twenty-five ropers at five dollars a day."

Red hot fury built behind his eyes. "Are you fixing to get replaced?"

Stan spit the toothpick out and lifted his head to stare at him. "I'd like to see you prove I done anything wrong." As Stan sauntered away, Conrad fumed. If he didn't learn to read fast, he'd lose everything, but not before he took care of Stan. Arnold came in, leading Lightning, one of their new geldings.

"Arnold, it's time we replaced Stan. I asked him to get feed and he got flour, I asked him to hire five men at a dollar a day, he hired twenty-five at five dollars."

Arnold's eyes went wide. "That's more than the foreman makes. Sakes alive, we'd better find them and weed out a few."

"Either way, it won't look good. Men who thought they had work, won't. And men who thought they were going to get rich, won't think much of the standard wage now. But The Broken Circle O will be bankrupt if we let him keep making these expensive mistakes."

Arnold nodded and leaned against the wall of a horse's stall. "I'd say, let's explain to them what happened. Stan did this, so he's got to take the blame for it. We'll keep six of the men, one to replace Stan and the five that we need. We can't do much about the pay. We just can't afford to pay ropers that much."

Conrad nodded. "I know I should've been the one to do those jobs. I shouldn't have asked Stan to do it, especially after the flour. I should've known he was up to something."

Arnold clapped him on the shoulder. "Being the boss is about delegating the work, just make sure you have Barton do those jobs from now on. His memory's like a steel trap."

He should have. And if he hadn't been so embarrassed, he would've. Soon, he wouldn't have to rely on anyone. Isabelle would teach him to read, and he'd be able to go into the lumber yard, the mercantile, or anywhere else. Even a bakery, if he had to.

Hours later, after going home to change and wash up, he strode into his parents' house, and the aroma that danced over his nose stopped him in his tracks. His ma could cook, he'd never questioned that, but nothing had ever come from her kitchen that smelled quite so compelling.

Conrad followed the luscious scent back to the kitchen to find Isabelle alone, bent over the stove. Though he didn't particularly want her to move, she was struggling with a heavy pot, and he couldn't leave her to get burned.

"Let me get that for you."

She jumped at the sound of his voice and dropped her apron onto the hot oven door. She shrieked and froze.

"Isabelle, get that out of the stove!" Conrad rushed to her, praying she didn't light herself ablaze, gripped her about the waist, and lifted her away from the stove. Her apron was scorched but didn't catch. He let her go and pulled the tie string of the apron, yanked it off, and threw it into the soapy wash bucket where her pans from baking the rolls were soaking.

Her face was pale, her eyes wide. Conrad grabbed two towels and lifted the roasting pans from the oven, closed it, and then faced Isabelle. A tear ran down her cheek.

He couldn't have that. Raising his voice had been out of fear, not anger. "Now, there's no cause for tears. I'm sorry I scared you. You just looked to be having some trouble with the pans."

"But I burned your ma's apron…"

"And she's likely got ten more. It isn't the first toasted apron around here, and I doubt it'll be the last." She still quivered on the verge of more tears, and he was out of ideas on how to stop them.

He wiped the stray damp trail from her cheek. "Now, is there anything else I can do, or should I just get my carcass out of your kitchen and leave you be?" He smiled, hoping she would, too.

Isabelle touched her hair, even though it wasn't a bit out of place. "I'll be fine. You don't have to stay in here with me. You can go out with your family, if you'd like."

He chuckled and leaned against the counter. "Well, in that case, I'd like to stay right here. The scenery's rather pretty and you can't beat the scent."

Finally, Isabelle laughed and the tension that had built inside him since he'd put his hands around her waist faded away. "I think I've found the poetry book I'd like you to start with. If it doesn't get too late tonight, will you have time?"

Ma and Pa entered the kitchen and Ma made herself busy gathering plates.

He didn't want to answer in front of his parents but couldn't leave her waiting for an answer. "If you're not too tired, I wouldn't mind spending a few extra minutes with you." He prayed she had time. Now that Stan was gone, he'd either have to trust his brothers as Arnold had suggested, or just learn. Once Isabelle found out, and he had a mind to tell her that night, she would help him. Never again would he do business without writing it down.

"I don't know why you say such things, Conrad," Isabelle said.

Maretta gave her son a lengthy look. "I think I know why he says such things. Conrad, you should speak to your father later." Her eyebrows rose and her lip was set into a hard line.

It was never a good idea to disagree with Ma. "Yes, ma'am."

"Maybe we should even do it now, before we sit down to eat?"

Pa would tell him to leave Isabelle alone, and though he knew he should, he didn't want to. Ma stood and led him from the room, gathering Pa with a slight tilt of her head. After thirty-two years of marriage, they could talk without speaking. To anyone around them, it was most unnerving.

Ma led them out to the paddock and leaned against the railing. He and Pa waited on either side for her to say what was on her mind. Ma would throttle you in a trice if you interrupted her.

"Conrad, that girl's only been here but a few days, and I can already see you fussing over her. But, fact is, she's a widow. Even if some people are getting away from mourning, her heart isn't ready for another man yet. And you're not ready to take on her grief when it finally hits her, and it will."

He knew it, she had to forget her first husband before there would ever be room for him, but that didn't mean he couldn't get close to her while she healed. She'd even mentioned Harland when they'd been out on their walk. She wasn't close to ready. "We aren't courting, Ma." Though if Isabelle would…

"It isn't that I don't think she's a good girl for you, dear. She's a fine woman. Just don't rush her too fast… she will break."

She was already broken, deeply, by that excuse of a man. "How long? I'm thirty-one years old. My youngest brother is already married and having children. I don't know how I know, but she's just…" His parents had always given sound advice, but even after only a few days, he thought about her all day, wanted to end work quickly so he could go see her. He wasn't getting any younger.

His pa finished his sentence better than he could have. "…perfect."

Conrad dipped his head. "How long, Pa?"

"Only she knows that. When she's able to share with you what happened, when she can laugh again, then she'll be ready."

Lula came out the front door and waved to them to let them know dinner was ready. After their meal, he'd get to spend a few minutes with Isabelle, if she was willing. That was an even better prospect than sweet rolls. But he couldn't court her. His parents were right. She would never love him without first healing from what her husband had done, and though Conrad didn't know exactly, her husband had done her bad. How he wished he could throttle that man.

CHAPTER 11

After the meal was cleared and Lula and Maretta set to doing the dishes, Izzy searched for Conrad. She found him in the midst of his brothers and father in the sitting room. Nathan, Conrad, and Arnold were all smoking their pipes while they relaxed, and Eli and Barton sat on a couch facing her. The talking stopped as she entered the room.

"I'm sorry to bother you." She bit her lip. Conrad had been so hesitant to let anyone know about his inability to read, she couldn't just ask for him to come and bring his book.

Conrad stood, rested his pipe on the mantle and led her out of the room.

"Where would you like to learn?" she whispered.

He smiled and put his hand on the small of her back, his touch gentle yet firm. "There's a small sun room on the south side of the house that Ma keeps flowers in. It gets powerful hot in there, but no one's liable to come and bother us."

No one would know they were there. Would he take advantage of the secluded room like Harland had? Izzy banished the thought. Conrad wouldn't. He was nothing like her husband and never would be. She had to stop worrying that all men were like her husband, when Conrad was showing her they weren't.

Conrad opened the door and they both went inside, shutting themselves off from the rest of the family. There was a small table in the center of the room that would be perfect for reading, or even for having tea, if she ever wanted to do such a thing again. A small leather-bound primer sat on the table, waiting. It was for children just learning to read.

The book had been flipped open to the first story and a picture of a boy playing fetch with a dog took up most of the first page. Conrad sat down in front of the book and waited for her to take her seat. When she did, he glanced up at her and reached for her hand. She didn't hesitate for even a moment before placing her fingers on his palm, and she reveled at the heat as it wove its way through her palm and up her arm.

"Isabelle, I… didn't really ask you here to teach me about poetry. I know a little, but I just never was able to…"

His hand gripped hers tighter and her heart ached for his pain. Lula had asked her not to shame him and she would've refused to anyway.

"You don't have to say it. I understand. I'll help you, just as I promised I would. Some people just have a harder time with it."

She slid her chair next to him. Though his size would be daunting to anyone else, to her it was now a comfort. Across the top of the first page she pointed to each letter and he knew them, then they steadily moved on to the sounds. After a few hours, she was tired and so was he. The lamp had burned low and the shadows were long, but he'd made so much progress, and her heart was full.

"Are you sorry you asked me for help?" Izzy pushed her chair from the table, and he laid his hand over hers, holding her there for a moment. Though the touch was intimate, even in its simplicity, she wouldn't deny that she craved it.

"I'm not. I know more now than I knew a few hours ago. If I didn't have to rise so early, I would stay with you longer."

Izzy stifled a yawn. She'd been up with the morning glories to get the rolls started. But had she not, she also would wish to stay longer.

"When you're ready, we can move on. Why don't you take the book with you and practice in the evenings until you're ready? I'll be here."

Conrad brushed his thumb over the top of her hand, sending a shiver up her arm.

"I've never been fond of teachers. I guess I didn't give them much credit. Thank you for proving me wrong."

Izzy laughed, a nervous lightning rod slashed within her. "I'm no teacher, Conrad." She took a step back from him to catch her breath and let her heart settle. The way he made her feel, at once safe and protected, was both sweet and simple. But when he touched her, she felt things she'd only felt once before, and it hadn't been half as potent then.

He stood and stretched his shoulders. "Why do you go by Izzy and not Isabelle?"

He'd called her that earlier, but she hadn't wanted to push him about why. It didn't really matter, she liked how the name sounded when he said it.

"There is no fun story, it's just what my parents called me, though, for a few years at the Normal School, I was Dizzy Izzy."

He frowned slightly. "My brother didn't call you that, did he? I'll wallop him." The threat dropped his voice to a low growl.

77

Her insides quivered deliciously at the sound. "Barton was too busy chasing after Lula to ever pester me."

"Well, *I'm* certainly not going to call you that. Would it bother you if I called you Isabelle?"

Though it was her true name, she'd come to dislike it. From anyone else, it would've given her pause, she may not even have answered. But not from him.

"If that's what you wish to call me, then do so." The space between them was fraught with dangerous questions neither of them were ready for, but she knew that to get closer to this man, she'd have to learn more about herself than she'd ever had to face.

"And might I call on you often?" His eyebrows rose, and he took a tentative step toward her.

He was getting too close to her heart. If he continued to ask her such questions, she would be tempted to let him into the secret cavern her heart had become, the place no one would want to venture.

"It's probably better for you if you don't."

He took another step closer to her and all the words she'd planned melted away.

"And why is that? Don't you want to spend time with me?" His wonderful lips tipped into a smile. Not the kind that portended a secret encounter, nor was it false in any way. It was warmth and honesty, and perhaps a dash of hope.

"I do want to spend time with you. I enjoyed our evening." But her heart was nowhere near ready. The dizzying sensations running around inside her were frightening after Harland had taken such advantage of those very feelings. She couldn't trust her traitorous heart.

"Then why can't I call on you often, if you enjoy my company so thoroughly?"

Her head pitched a warning. She had no business feeling

anything for anyone. "I'm just a poor widow. I have nothing to offer you, Conrad."

His hand slid out from his side and grasped hers once again. "At my age, I'm fairly certain of the things I want. I know the foods I like, and those I don't. I know which seasons I care for, and which I'm happy to see gone. I know green is green, and I know better than anyone how to run this ranch. So, when I say that I want to call on you more often, it's because I already know that's what I want. I'm also gentlemanly enough to give you the choice. If that's how you feel, then I'll see you in a few days for another lesson."

He released her and flipped the book closed. She couldn't let him leave, not like that. She stepped in his way as he turned for the door and the wall of his chest crashed into her.

She stepped back, forcing her breath back into lungs too shocked to work as her gaze took far too long to amble up his broad chest to his thick neck, with his hint of whiskers this late in the evening, up to his neat mustache and, finally, eyes that burned hot as they took her in just as she'd done to him.

"I... I want to be the woman who welcomes a visit. But every time you come near me, I hear his voice inside my head telling me I'm everything horrible under the sun."

Conrad traced his finger from her temple down to her chin, sending a delicious shiver down her spine. His intense gaze was too much, and she closed her eyes to escape it.

"Just by telling me that, you're getting stronger, Isabelle. I'm proud of you." He leaned forward and his lips brushed her forehead, warm and reassuring. She clutched his vest and he froze.

"Don't go." No one had ever been so tender with her, and she couldn't let the moment slip away. "Please. Don't go."

He wrapped his strong arms around her waist and she laid her head against his chest, listening to his steady heartbeat as his words caressed her soul. *I'm proud of you.*

His heart wasn't beating half as erratically as hers. He pressed his lips to her forehead again and again, and just held her there. All the hurt poured from her in silent soft tears, and Conrad didn't say a word. When her tears finally stopped, she pulled away from him. He caressed her face, wiping the dampness from her cheeks.

"I don't want to leave you, but I've got to." He gently drew her face closer and held her once again. "I meant what I said. I know what I want, and I want to spend time with you."

For the first time in months, the rattling voice in her head was silent, and so she listened to her heart. "Then I think you should."

His mouth slowly came down over hers. It was a simple caress of lips, just a taste. He didn't push her for more.

"Sleep well. I'll see you tomorrow, not because I'll need another lesson, but because I will want to see you."

He left her there, heart fluttering and totally speechless. *I'm proud of you* was the most powerful thing anyone had ever said to her, and she ached to hear it again.

CHAPTER 12

The next night, Conrad lit his lamp at the small table in his cabin and pulled out the little reader. The letters were still the same, but his mind struggled to come up with the sounds. As his finger traveled along the line like Isabelle had shown him, he couldn't produce the words as he had before. It had been so much easier with Isabelle there, when he'd had to get the answer right to see her smile at him. Though he wanted to learn for his own good, there was no immediate benefit without her.

The lamp wasn't bright enough, the table not right, he couldn't focus. Would Isabelle think less of him if he went to her and asked for her to just sit with him while he worked? She said she believed in his ability, had convinced him he wasn't as muddled as he felt. So why was he back to the same problems when she wasn't there?

He slid a slip of cut tin in to hold his place and closed the book. He turned down the lamp, resolved to leave his cabin and go see her. The book fit easily in his vest pocket. His cabin wasn't far from the house, and if he hurried, Isabelle would still be sitting in the front room, reading. Hastening across the open area between the shelter wall of the bull pen and the machine shed, he slid through the dark expanse as quietly as possible.

Stan slithered from the shadows and stood in front of him, his hand cradled at his waist, just inches from his barker.

"You made me lose my job. How am I supposed to find another one out here? Doesn't my family matter to you? Or is your family the only thing on your mind lately. You big, dumb oaf."

Conrad measured the distance out of the alley between the two buildings. Letting Stan's words get to him would only cloud his judgment. "You did the damage yourself, Stan. You had a good place here. Lots of freedom and plenty of trust, but you broke that. You know darn well I didn't call for flour. I wouldn't even ask you to buy foodstuff for the house. It isn't your job. And twenty-five men... at five dollars a day? You know what our going wages are and that's not it."

Stan snickered in the shadows. "I said it yesterday, I'll say it again. Prove it."

His dedication to keep Stan from getting to him was fast dissolving. "We live by our word out here, Stan. That musta bothered you. It's time for you to go somewhere where they'll bend the way you want. That place isn't here. You should've cleared your things out earlier. You need to git. Now."

"You live by your word? That's a good yarn." Stan spat and squinted at Conrad in the near darkness. "Wonder if all those men your brother sent home today are saying you live by your word?"

"They wouldn't be saying anything if you hadn't tricked

them. That was all on you." Conrad didn't want to scuffle with the man. He wasn't worried about besting him, but he didn't want to go see Isabelle after a fight. He was also tired of wasting his time shooting the breeze between the barns with Stan, who wouldn't listen to him anyway. There was a lovely lady waiting for him, Stan was a waste of precious time.

"See, now." Stan chuckled. "They don't feel tricked by *me*. They feel taken by *you*."

Conrad reached for his gun, but he'd taken it off when he'd come in from the range that evening, and he hadn't thought he'd need it to see Isabelle.

"Now, isn't that a shame. Caught empty-handed." Stan sneered. "Not much of a cowboy, getting caught without your irons."

Three more men crept from the darkness. None of them were visible in the shadows. Every muscle in his arm flexed in readiness. Four to one. It was only one more than when he'd taken on all his brothers. It could be done, as long as they played fair.

One of the men furthest from him drew in the blink of an eye, and Conrad only had a moment to think before he saw the bright flash and felt the back of his head crack against the hard dirt.

THE BOOK DIDN'T HOLD her interest in the slightest. Wordsworth just wasn't compelling in all his talk of life as normal when her heart was ready to believe life was anything but. Conrad wanted to spend time with her, to call on her. Now that she'd been a married woman, she didn't have to seek permission from her parents or the approval of anyone else. The freedom was a giddiness that wouldn't be contained.

She'd hoped that he would still come by yet. He'd gone home to sup that evening instead of coming to the house. That was his normal routine, so it shouldn't bother her. But it wasn't as if she could go to *his* cabin and eat. Unless he invited her. Her heart clenched in her chest at the thought. No, even a widow had no business stepping into the cabin of a single man.

A shot pierced the night and Izzy fairly jumped out of her skin. In the few days she'd been to the ranch, she hadn't heard the report of a gun, and coming so late in the evening when the shooter couldn't see to aim…

Nathan ran down the stairs, tugging his braces over his shoulders. He reached for the rifle over the door and ran into the night. Izzy stared out the window, too frightened to think about her own safety. Someone out there could be hurt. Someone like Conrad. Barton would be at his home with Lula. She'd been more tired the closer she came to her time. They wouldn't have left their house. Arnold and Eli were both at their homes and, as far as she knew, didn't walk about at night. But Conrad did. He'd been out almost every evening. A sick dread took over her stomach.

Within a few moments, three of the brothers wandered into the front. It was too dark to tell for sure who they were, but not a one of them looked big enough to be the bear that was Conrad.

All three men met their father in the darkness between two of the barns, barely discernible in the dark. When they reappeared, two balanced the weight of large shoulders, while one carried the feet. Nathan held his gun and led the way. He was too big to be anyone but Conrad. She choked back a sob. He couldn't be dead, not now, not when she'd just started looking to him and seeing hope in a future.

Barton had Conrad's boots, one in each hand, and Izzy rushed to the door to hold it open as they brought Conrad in. His eyes were open but unfocused. She searched him for any sign of blood, but there was none that she could see. They flopped him onto the sofa and the breath whooshed from his chest. Isabelle knelt on the floor beside him and reined in her fear. He was still with her, even awake, she should be overjoyed, but the distant look in his eyes was no reassurance.

Nathan stood behind her. "I found him between the barns. There was no one out there by the time I got there. Hopefully, he'll be able to tell us what happened."

There was an area of black on his vest, right over his heart. She touched it and found a hole. As she lifted the vest, she found the primer she'd given him the night before and pulled it from the wide pocket. He'd placed it in his vest with the front of the book facing him and a cut piece of tin to keep his place in the front of the book where they'd left off. The whole of the book and the tin absorbed the shot, and the bullet lay wedged in the pages.

Nathan took it from her and she shuddered at how closely she'd come to losing Conrad. Izzy wrapped her arm around him as best she could and rested her head against his heart. The cadence just as calming as it had been the evening before when she'd bared her heart and he'd held her anyway. Now he needed her.

Conrad ran shaking fingers through her hair, but his hold was weak and soon his hand fell at his side, and he slept. His brothers and father retired to another room, but Izzy couldn't leave him alone. When he woke, he'd still be in that moment, just before he was shot. If it were her laying there, she would want someone with her, to calm her. If it were her, she would want him to do the same for her. She rested her head on his chest once more and let the rise and fall lull her as she held him.

CHAPTER 13

His chest ached with every breath, like his insides were stretched. But he was alive. The shot hadn't killed him. No way, Heaven hurt this bad. He reached for his chest to rub the ache and buried his hand in soft hair. His eyes flew open and the top of Isabelle's head was all he could see. She was either holding her breath, or he was sadly mistaken and Heaven hurt *a lot* more than he thought.

She slowly untangled his hand from her hair and sat up, staring at him for a minute. She didn't release him, but instead wove her fingers through his. The gentle softness was just what he needed when the last thing he could remember seeing was the flash of a bullet.

"Do you know what happened?" she asked quietly.

He glanced quickly around the room and they were alone, their only companion that of the weak lamp on a nearby table. Isabelle was bathed in soft, golden light, her cheeks flushed from where she'd been lying against him. He'd never seen anything quite so beautiful as this woman, rumpled because she'd been sleeping on him.

"Stan. He wanted revenge."

Isabelle let go of him and lifted something from the floor where she knelt, revealing his book, a gaping hole now marring the green canvas sheathing of the hardback cover.

"It saved your life. If you hadn't come to me and asked me to teach you…" She shuddered, and he reached for her. Instead of coming back to his arms as he'd hoped, she wove her fingers within his. Though it was closeness he desired, he wanted to hold *her* close, not just her hand.

"I'm sorry. You must think me silly to get so emotional when we've only just met. It's just that… except Lula, I have no one else. My family loved Harland, thought there was none better for me. They don't know I'm here." Her face tilted down and she dabbed at her nose with a kerchief hidden in the folds of her skirt. "They would probably be quite saddened by his loss. I should've told them. I shouldn't have been so afraid to go to them."

He pressed her hand slightly, hoping she would continue so the trust between them could grow.

"I don't think you're silly at all. If you hadn't chosen to come here, my brothers would be digging a hole for me today." He shifted, and his chest was on fire with the ache of a deep bruise. "You've lost your husband, and even if you fell away from him, you must have loved him once. At least enough to follow him down the aisle. You can write to your family if it would make you feel better… or less alone." He'd promised to help her with the bakery, and even though he didn't want her to be in town, away from him, he'd do it if the success of the business would help her believe in her own value.

She met his gaze. "I don't feel so alone… when I'm with you."

How could he help but smile at that admission? He squeezed her hand again, unsure of what else he should say. Sentiment, like poetry, was a language he'd never learned.

He wanted to kiss her, to fill her ears with those flowery words she longed to hear, but how was a man to learn such things? He drew her hand to his lips and trailed kisses from her knuckles to her wrist, then flipped her hand and placed one more where her pulse beat franticly.

"Isabelle, can you bring my pa and my brothers back in here?"

She nodded and loosed his hand, but he didn't let go as she stood. "Thank you for staying with me, Isabelle. Waking up to a friendly face is about the most pleasant thing a man could ask for."

She blushed a pretty red and only then did he realize his words might have another meaning. He released her hand as she dashed from the room. He picked up the book where she'd left it on his chest. It was destroyed, the bullet had gone through the back and all the way to his tin marker at about the twentieth page. He wouldn't be able to use it anymore. Shame burned him clear through. Now his brothers would know his secret.

Pa, Barton, Eli, and Arnold came and sat around the sofa as Conrad pushed himself up to sitting, forcing his muscles to do what they didn't want to. Isabelle was nowhere in sight. He'd scared her off with his poorly chosen words.

Barton crossed his arms over his chest. "Izzy told us it was Stan. We'll have to get the law involved. If he's taken a shot at you, it's too dangerous to handle on our own."

Conrad shifted and massaged the aching muscle between his chest and abdomen. "It wasn't Stan himself, it was someone with him. And just what do we tell them? It's his word against mine. I couldn't see the guys who were with him, but I'd bet every last one of them would testify Stan was with them somewhere far from the Broken Circle O when it happened."

Eli pounded his fist into his hand. "We can't just let him get away with this. We shouldn't have to use our men to patrol our land."

They didn't have enough men for that. "We don't even know if the men we kept on are loyal. They might still side with Stan. They were told they'd get five dollars a day, that's a lot higher than what they're actually getting now."

Barton tipped his head. "So, what do we do? I don't want murderous men sneaking around when my wife could have her baby any day."

Eli shoved to his feet and stomped to the other side of the room. "Is that all you think about, Barton? You're married. That doesn't make the rest of this operation *less* important. We've all got a stake in it. I'd think the possibility of a new generation of Olesons would make you want to protect your land more."

"I do want to protect it, but not because of the land. I don't want anything to happen to my wife, my family. I can go buy land anywhere. I'll never find another Lula."

Not so long ago, Conrad would've scoffed, thinking his brother was weak. Now, after experiencing the immediate pull the right woman could have, it didn't seem so crazy. He didn't want Stan around when Isabelle could be caught in the fire, either.

THAT STRANGE FLUTTERING in her belly reminded her of the nerves she'd felt at first with Harland, when he was still trying to woo her with words. Because Conrad was right, there had been a time when she'd allowed herself to enjoy Harland's company, to feel beautiful when he paid her words of sweetness. No matter how false they'd been. It was only after they'd wed, and he'd been so disappointed, that the hurt began.

The pleasant thrumming through her belly had only lasted with Harland a short time, but did that mean it would be the same with Conrad? Would he tire of her company? He didn't find her *big*, as Harland had, at least that wouldn't stand in their way. But were all couples destined to fade to separate bedrooms, and a painful silence only punctuated by biting words too hard to forget?

The house felt empty with Maretta abed and the men all situated and talking in the front room. Her thoughts were far too active to let her sleep, yet there was no one to talk with. She roamed to the kitchen and began pulling out the reserve jar of flour, the yeast, and buttermilk. The recipe didn't matter, she just needed to be busy.

After she'd rolled out the dough and sprinkled on the cinnamon and brown sugar mixture, a shadow fell across the counter next to her. She turned to find Conrad leaning against the doorframe staring at her.

She tried to catch her breath, but her words failed. Just the sight of him gave her gooseflesh.

"Isabelle, what are you doing roaming about at this hour?" He tilted his head, his face drawn with concern.

Irrational worry built up in her chest. Had she done something wrong? Maybe he really did think her big and she shouldn't be in the kitchen at all... "I couldn't sleep." Partly because she hadn't even tried.

"Did my careless words bother you so much that I kept you from rest?"

Careless? She'd thought them rather frank, but it hadn't been his words, but thoughts of *what if* that had driven her to the kitchen. "No, I just wanted a few minutes to think."

"You left me two hours ago. That's a lot of minutes. Have you worked out what you needed to?" He was so relaxed, standing there in the doorway, not hovering over her, wondering about her every move. Curious, not controlling. He hadn't even asked her why she was there, just why she was up.

She looked down at her work. The rolls just needed to be cut and then put into the oven.

"No, I'm not quite done yet."

He strode into the room and pulled a chair over to the counter where she was working. His nearness as he sat next to her rekindled all the feelings she'd just been worrying over. He reached for her hand and ran his fingers down hers. How did he know she craved his touch?

"I don't think I've felt hands so soft before..."

She made to tug away, but he laughed softly and held fast.

"Are you insinuating that I don't work?" She forced herself to sound huffy, but it was a show. The pleasantness of his warm hand over hers overshadowed all other feelings. He traced her fingers gently, and she wanted to pull away from him, to get away from all the feelings, sweet as they were.

"I would never say such an untruth. You're trembling. Do I frighten you?"

Yes... and no. "I'm terrified that this pull I feel for you will be as short-lived as the first time I felt it. That I'll let myself be weak to you and end up broken once again. It isn't you I fear. It's me."

Conrad stopped his finger from its soft conquest of hers and let his hand wind up her arm to her elbow then behind her, and then he drew her to him. The solid wall of his chest was more of a comfort than anything she'd known before. His vest was charred right over his heart and the smell brought back all the terror she'd driven to the back of her mind. She clung to him as the tears fell. She'd almost lost him.

"I will not turn you away, Isabelle. Never. I want you closer to me, always nearer. I'm not a man of pretty words. Falsehoods are dastardly, and you won't hear them from me."

His hand caressed her cheek and tipped her chin as he ran his thumb over the tender skin of her lips. "I want to kiss you, but if you believe, even a little, that I'm being false. I won't."

True to his word, he held her in place. His mouth descended no further, but she was torn between her desire for real affection and passion, yet trapped by her fear.

"I…" *want you, I need you, but I can't say the words, and I'm so afraid…*

Where he sat on the stool, she would only have to take one step and complete the kiss, if she could force her body forward. He sighed and closed his eyes as she dipped, advancing on him. Their lips met and she parted quickly, leaving him suddenly wide-eyed.

"I need to finish my rolls." She laughed, nervous as she tried to escape his hold.

He wound his hand back into her hair as it had been when he woke earlier and, in the space of a heartbeat, he gently drew her around and kissed her once again, obliterating any likeness she could place between Conrad and Harland. From that moment on, Harland was well and truly dead. Her heart hammered in her chest and there was nothing but his lips and hers.

When he parted from her and tucked her tenderly under

his chin, she knew, beyond all doubt, that what he said had been the truth. He would never cast her away.

"I'm about to say something just as careless as I did before, but I find that with you, I can speak my mind. I could fall asleep every night to that and not tire of it."

Though it embarrassed her to admit it, she had to agree.

CHAPTER 14

Morning came on turtle's feet as Izzy shoved her arms into her borrowed house coat. Though she'd been kissed before, it was as if Conrad's had torn all others from her memory and burned them to bits. Lula had told her that Barton admitted he'd loved her from the moment he'd set eyes on her, and now Izzy knew that could be true. It was as if the Lord had whispered to her, *Conrad was the one I wanted for you, dear child,* and it was foolish to refuse.

As she tugged her stays in place and tied them, she caught her reflection in the glass. A year and a half ago, she'd had a rounded bosom and more thickness about her middle, which had curved down to more shapely hips. Now, she was narrow from head to toe. Strange that she'd found herself pretty then, but not as much now after becoming the woman her husband had wanted her to be. Even after she'd changed as he'd wished, he'd never really wanted her again, anyway. Only the few times he'd been too broke or couldn't sell anything to visit the saloon, had he touched her. Until her husband had told her she shouldn't be pleased with her appearance, she had been. In the time she'd been at the ranch, she'd gained back a little of what she'd lost, and she rested her hands on the slight indent at her waist.

It was time to let go of everything he'd done and said. He was never going to be sorry; he'd died without so much as looking at her. She'd chosen to marry him and now he was gone. Izzy smiled as she slid her blue dress over her head. She *wasn't* big, not anymore. Maybe she never had been. Conrad had claimed Harland was a liar, and those were words she could believe in.

Her Bible lay on her bedside table, and she flipped it open to the letter her mother had sent her when she'd first become a wife, the one telling her to be happy with her husband, and she tossed it into the burn basket. She was free to write her mother, free to say what she liked, free to accept Conrad's court, if he asked her. *Free.*

No one would miss her if she took a few minutes to write the letter she should've written before she'd left Tinton. And it was past time to face her mother. Words flowed onto the paper as she detailed Harland's passing and what he'd done to her. The letter was soon two full pages, and Izzy scanned the text to be sure she hadn't missed anything, nor misrepresented anything. Her mother would be sorely hurt by the missive, but if her family loved her, they would accept her. She held the cedar pencil aloft for just a moment, then signed, *Isabelle Harmon.* Her family name was better than the one she'd married into, and the name Conrad had chosen to call her sounded better to her ears. She didn't want to be Izzy Lawson anymore.

Maretta flung her door wide and Isabelle gasped, clutching at her hair still in a plait down her shoulder.

"Izzy, Lula needs you. It's time!"

Time… She hadn't prepared! It was still almost a month early. Even now, her heart ached at the thought of watching Lula give birth when *she* should've just been filling out with her own bundle. But that couldn't be changed. Harland had taken one thing from her too precious to ever forget, but Harland was gone, and the only one who could put salve on that wound, was the Lord.

"I'm coming." She left the letter on her desk and flung her hair over her shoulder as she rushed from the room.

Barton and Lula's home was about a quarter mile away, south of his parents'. Maretta led the way as Isabelle had never been there. Barton's horse waited, saddled, right outside the front door.

"He came and got me. The doctor's not in town today."

The words chilled her through the July heat. They wouldn't be able to fall back on the doctor, she'd have to do it alone. The fear nipped at her resolve, but there was no one else. Her only friend needed her. "And have you attended a birthing before?" Isabelle huffed as she pushed harder to reach the house.

"Only my own." Maretta sagged slightly as they reached the door. Barton opened it and pulled his mother inside, Isabelle followed quickly.

He raked his hand through his hair. "She's hurting. You've got to do something."

Maretta patted her son's shoulder. "That's the way of it, Barton. A woman isn't like a cow or a horse. Remember your scriptures, Son."

Isabelle couldn't possibly forget. *And women will have pain in childbirth…* Lula moaned loudly from behind a door somewhere down a short hall. Barton led her to their room, and she swallowed hard, setting her shoulders and fortifying her spine before she stepped inside.

Lula's knees were up, though she was under a sheet, and her head swung slowly from side to side as she moaned. Terrible noises, the likes of which Isabelle had never heard before, shook her to her very core.

"Lula, I'm here," Isabelle said as she approached the bed.

Lula glanced up, her face crimson and puckered as she curled forward. "I don't know what to do, and I wasn't ready for this. I've got another month. Isn't there a way to make it stop?"

Isabelle gripped her fingers. "If there is, I surely don't know it. I think we've just got to get the work done."

Lula groaned again and threw her head back into the pillow, arching her back. "I can't do this, I just can't. I want my sisters here, my mother…" Lula gasped and balled up again, clamping her mouth shut.

"I'm going to go get towels and the like. I'll send Barton in with you until I get back."

Lula shook her head. "No, don't. The poor man is terrified, and it makes it worse. Just hurry back."

Instead of sending Barton, she met Maretta at the door. The older woman had already collected towels and water. A set of sewing scissors was tucked in the tie of her apron. That was something Isabelle hadn't thought of, and a job she wouldn't offer to do. Maretta handed Isabelle an apron and eased past her.

"I'll get Lula comfortable on some towels and sheets, you get that man out of the house. He's about fit to burst with nothing to do but worry, and he won't listen to his ma."

Isabelle closed the bedroom door and found Barton sitting at the kitchen table, his head cradled in his hands. She sat with him and took a deep breath. Everything would be better if she could leave, be anywhere but there, but Lula needed her. Someday, she prayed fervently, Lula could return the favor and be there for *her* birthing.

"Barton, you can't stay here. Listening to her will drive you mad. Go out and work for a while. We'll be here. There's nothing you can do for her."

He tipped his head to glance at her. "She said that her sister Jennie only ever labored with her husband, doesn't she want me in there with her?"

The truth was always best, but hurting a man when he was already down was just plain mean. "Her sister's husband knew just how to help her because they had planned for it. He wasn't worried for his wife. Can you say the same?"

Barton's head plunged back into his hands. "No. I can't. I never want to see Lula hurting, and this was my fault."

Poor man. She laid what she hoped was a reassuring hand on his arm. "Barton, she is your wife, this isn't your *fault*, it's a blessing."

As Conrad came in, Isabelle jumped to her feet away from Barton. She smiled at him for a moment but leaned forward for her words to only reach Barton's ears. "Besides, I'm sure Lula had no part in it, whatsoever."

Barton's head shot up, his eyes wide at her jest.

"Now, go with your brother and get something done. We've got work to do here."

Whether it was the shock of what she'd said, or his brother's presence, she didn't know. Something motivated him to stand and stomp outside, leaving Isabelle alone with Conrad.

He strode toward her and took in every inch of her face as he brushed her braid over her shoulder. "You look terrified."

Her heart hadn't slowed since Maretta had busted into her room earlier. "I am."

Conrad took a step closer to her and held her for a moment, which was far too short. "You're just here to help your friend. The work is up to Lula. Pray for her and the little mite, and I'll check on you later." He bent and brushed his lips over the top of her head, then followed Barton out of the house.

Lula screamed and Maretta called for Isabelle, and her insides clenched once again. The situation had been much easier to consider while Conrad had held her. Isabelle rushed back into the room as Lula arched her back and yelled. A few minutes later, Maretta cut the cord on a baby boy.

While Maretta cleaned up the bawling baby, she tasked Isabelle to wait for the afterbirth. But, after a few more pains, it was obvious Lula wasn't finished. Fifteen minutes later, Maretta cut the cord on her granddaughter. This time, she handed the baby to Isabelle to wash up while she stayed with Lula.

The baby was ruddy, its movements jerky and cry strong. She had a fuzz of blonde hair all over the top of her perfect, tiny head. Isabelle was immediately in love with the child. Isabelle's desire to have her own grew with each moment of holding the precious newborn until she thought the ache would never subside.

After Lula was washed down and the bedding changed, she cuddled both children close to her. "Now, I want Barton to be here. I would guess he went out on the range and won't be back until supper. Do you suppose he'll expect me to cook?" Her eyes were wide, and she held her bundled children a little tighter.

Maretta laughed. "Men don't quite understand the work that just one of those tiny babies can bring. I will get a pot of stew started you both can eat from as you're hungry. Izzy can come by each day and help if you need it."

Isabelle smiled and ran her finger over the soft tufts of hair on the baby girl's head. "I can. They are beautiful, Lula. Do you have names picked for them?"

Lula laid the little girl on the bed, then the boy next to her. "We'd picked out a name for both a boy and a girl, but we'd never thought we might need them both. I'd like to check with Barton before we tell anyone."

The babies wiggled slightly in their sleep, but stilled quickly, curling against one another. Isabelle brushed a lock of damp, curly blonde hair from Lula's face. "I need to go find Conrad. I'll send Barton back here when I find him. I would suspect they're together."

Lula nodded but didn't look up. Her attention was completely taken with her new family, and another ache built in Isabelle's chest. She would have to wait for her own precious blessings. Before she could even allow herself to consider children, she had to convince a certain cowboy that she was ready for his suit.

As CONRAD RODE toward the barn, Barton close behind, he caught sight of Isabelle, her blue dress waving softly in the breeze as she waited for them. Barton saw her just a moment later and kicked Star to a run.

If Isabelle were worried, she wouldn't be standing so calmly, waiting for them. But part of him wanted to spur Talon to a run, too, just to get to her quicker. Barton dismounted and, as Conrad rode up and reined in, Barton dropped to his knees. Conrad was off his horse in a flash, and he ran just as Barton returned to his feet.

"Twins…" Barton breathed.

"Two?" Conrad glanced to Isabelle, and her radiant smile about had him falling just like Barton.

"Twins," she confirmed. "Now, you need to get home and help her name them."

Barton reached for his mount and was gone in seconds. Though they were standing in the middle of the open, he felt alone with her. Isabelle searched his face for a moment, then stepped toward him. He loved how she was always closing the gap between them.

"That was all at once terrifying and beautiful." She paused as pain crossed over her pretty blue eyes. "I did it, Conrad. I didn't think I could watch her, not after what *he* did to me, but I did. Now my heart aches all the more for what I lost."

A sick dread struck him and he opened his arms to her. She sighed and crushed herself to him. The tiny woman was stronger than she looked, and he cradled her there, never wanting to let her go, but knowing he must until she was ready.

"Isabelle, I told you I'd never send you away, and I mean it. You can take all the time you need to heal."

Her body shuddered, but it was her words that cut him deep into his heart.

"He killed my baby, Conrad. I would've gladly taken his words on my shoulders every day for the rest of my life if he'd just left our baby alone."

He tightened his grip around her, but words failed him. There was nothing he could do. Harland was already dead and words wouldn't amount to much of anything.

"You've lived through more than some women will ever face, and you've come out stronger for it. I don't know what the purpose was, or if you were ever meant to be with him at all, but I do know you were meant to be here, now, with me. I feel it right down to my bones."

She glanced up at him, and he wanted to kiss her, to chase all the hurt from her eyes.

"I know. I feel the same, and that's why I wrote a letter to my mother this morning. Would you take me into Belle Fourche to mail it? I'd also like to see this building Maretta told me about. It might make a good bakery. I've decided I'm staying in Belle Fourche."

Town was too far away to go every day, and he wanted her nearby whenever he had a mind to see her... for the rest of his life.

"Only if you want to. You'll be busy for the next while helping Lula, and if you're really looking for someone to bake for... I know a guy who's always hungry..."

She laughed, and the change that came over her face was a beauty to behold.

"I don't have to start a bakery, but I do want something. Do you think baking for this hungry man would take up my time? Would I feel accomplished at the end of the day?"

"Hmmm..." He tilted his head and smiled. "He might not eat enough to keep you cooking *all* day, but his house might need a little sprucing up, and his sister-in-law definitely needs help for a while."

She swatted his shoulder. "Are you hiring me as a housekeeper for Arnold?" Her lips tilted up slightly in an impertinent grin. Oh, how he loved her spunk.

He shook his head and adored the surprised sweet 'o' of her lips as he dipped his head to taste them. It was only a moment, just a sample, but he couldn't wait a moment longer.

"No. I'm asking you to stay here, on this ranch, with me. Stay here until you're ready to walk down the aisle to me. I can be the man *he* never was. I want to give you the sun and moon and everything in between."

Isabelle stared at him for a moment, the stunned 'o' of her lips still in place as a tear rolled down her cheek.

"And you said you weren't one for pretty words… I think that's the most beautiful poetry I've ever heard."

CHAPTER 15

After two weeks of working every evening from a primer, Conrad could read well enough to get by. Isabelle had borrowed it from the new teacher at the Belle Fourche school where Lula used to teach. It turned out his mind had wanted the exercise and, with such a pleasant teacher, the work had gone quickly—when he wasn't trying to steal a kiss for every little success.

He was now ready to start into his second book. She'd mentioned to him that she was ready to think about the bakery, but he hadn't wanted to talk about it. After a few weeks of having her all to himself, he didn't want to give her up all day. But her desire to do *something* to fill a deep need within her to be busier than anyone else, was so strong he could feel it coursing through her when he held her close.

After a short knock on Conrad's door, Isabelle came in and left the door open. She grew prettier by the day. Even in her plain calico, she was a beauty. He stood from his place at the table where he'd been practicing ahead of time. There was a nervousness about her, in the way she stood a bit off, and her glance never quite lit on him.

"Conrad… My parents are here. They've come to take me home."

He shoved his chair, sending it to the floor and making her flinch away from him. "No!" The word escaped before he could stop it. But he couldn't dictate her whereabouts any more than her parents could. She was a woman with her own mind. "Unless, you want to go." Why wouldn't she look at him?

She shook her head and stepped forward, finally gazing up at him. "I don't know what to say. I don't want to be disrespectful… but they don't understand."

He didn't understand, either. "Do they know? Did you tell them that we'll be married when the time is right?"

She shook her head. "I wrote the letter before you asked me. It was only about Harland's death, and I finally told them the truth about everything he'd done."

He couldn't keep from touching her any more than he could keep from blinking. He pulled her close and pressed a gentle kiss to the top of her head; the perfect spot when she was in his arms. "They may be here thinking you need to be at home in your grief. We'll tell them together."

Isabelle shook her head and drew away from him. "No, you don't understand. They loved him. They were so angry when they saw I wasn't in mourning. They came because I signed my letter with my maiden name. I don't want any part of him anymore."

"They didn't believe you, or they just think mourning is appropriate since you're a widow?" He couldn't quite understand how her parents could side with a man who'd done nothing but hurt their only daughter.

"I don't know." She rested her forehead against his chest. "I just know that I don't want to go with them. I wasn't allowed to be in mourning for my child, and I won't mourn the man who killed it."

The answer seemed obvious to him, but would she see it that way? She was the same age as Barton, twenty-one, and her parents had no legal stand to control her.

"Isabelle. They can't make you do anything you don't want to. You already know I want you here, with me, but I can't make you stay any more than they can make you go. The choice is yours."

She gently ran her hand up and down his chest, then paused over his heart. "I've never wanted to be anywhere more than I want to be right here, with you. I'm meant to be with you."

"Then let's go talk to them, together."

He turned and led her from the house. As he turned to close the door, a bullet whizzed by his head and lodged in the door frame. Isabelle screamed, and he grabbed for her, but she ran as another shot cracked in the distance. He slammed to his belly to make himself a harder target. Isabelle slipped into the nearest barn, and he sighed his relief that she was no longer out in the open. He could focus without her in the line of fire.

As he searched the rolling hills for any sign of the shooter, he held his breath. They hadn't seen any sign of Stan for weeks. Arnold peered out from the corner of the bull pen shelter and pointed toward the main house. The shooter was smart. None of them would ever return fire at their parents' home. Not when they knew Ma was in there. He scanned the flower beds and corners, but nothing moved and there were no more shots.

Conrad got to his feet, crouching low as he ran, and met his brother in the cover of the machine shed. "What was all that about?"

Arnold shook his head. "Don't know, but I'm guessing Stan or one of his friends is back. He only aimed at you, not at Izzy or me, and we were both in plain sight when the shots started."

They strode for the house as two people came out the front door, followed by Ma. "Boys, what's going on out here?" She glared at them as if they were children horsing around.

Arnold ignored her question and parted the short bush at the front corner of the house. He bent down and held up a shell casing. "Here's where he was hiding. He had to have slipped away, back around the house. He could be anywhere now."

"Isabelle..." Conrad spun around and searched for her. She hadn't come out of the barn yet, and he prayed it was only because she was still terrified.

"Wait!" The man on the porch yelled.

Conrad gritted his teeth and stopped. He turned back to the man as he came down the stairs. He needed to know Isabelle was safe and waiting built a fury in him that was hard to contain.

"I'm Nelson Harmon, Izzy's father. I'd like to come with you."

Conrad nodded, but only because he wanted to get going and find Isabelle. He strode toward the barn, leaving the older man to follow. Mr. Harmon remained silent as Conrad slipped through the door. He'd hoped Isabelle would be right out where they could see her, waiting for him, but a frightened woman might go anywhere.

He softly called for her, not wanting to scare her further. "Isabelle?"

Mr. Harmon started searching the pens, and Conrad went to the loft ladder. He wouldn't have chosen it as a hiding place himself; in a gunfight it would trap you in position, but Isabelle wouldn't know that. Once in the loft, he searched through all the hay and the area wired off for chickens. She wasn't there.

The ladder was a waste of precious time and he jumped from the loft back down to the barn. Mr. Harmon met him there.

"She isn't in here. You're sure this is where you saw her run?"

He nodded and strode for the back door. A slip of paper lay on the ground. He growled as he swiped it up.

Time for a trade.

Mr. Harmon glanced over Conrad's shoulder at the note. "What does it mean?"

He crumpled the sheet into his fist. "It means Stan wants to die."

THE LITTLE SCHOOLHOUSE wasn't as welcoming as when she'd borrowed the books for Conrad. Isabelle lay huddled against the wall where her captor had tossed her. Next to her, the new teacher cowered, clinging to her. She was young and terrified, fresh from the Normal School in Spearfish.

Isabelle had gathered, from his ranting, that the man who held them was Stan, the man who'd cornered Conrad between the barns. His buddy was supposed to have taken care of Conrad for good, but the shot didn't *take*. She wasn't about to tell him his friend's aim had been true. Conrad had been saved by the hand of God. And hopefully His hand was over her, and the new teacher, as well.

Stan paced the front of the classroom, intermittently

scratching his chin and rubbing his hands together in barely contained glee.

"I wrote a note. A note! The simpleton can't read it. He'll be so worried about you that he'll have to ask someone for help. It was one easy sentence and he'll have to ask for help. Then everyone will know." His breathing came faster as he spoke, and he squeaked as he laughed. His building agitation pushed her closer to the wall, as small as she could make herself. If he didn't notice either of them, he would stay over there, far from them. The more he spoke, the more she was sure he wasn't in his right mind, and that terrified her.

The blonde next to her whispered prayers with her eyes locked tightly shut. Stan hadn't told her what he'd planned for them, but it couldn't be good. They had seen his face, and she knew his intent for Conrad. He couldn't let her go and hope to get away. If she kept her wits, she might be able to do some good before he killed her. She might be able to prevent Stan from killing Conrad. As long as Conrad made it, that was all that mattered.

Stan bore down on her and stared with wide eyes. His hair hadn't been trimmed in quite some time, and his beard had grown in uneven, giving him the look of a squatter.

"It might take a bit for him to get the courage to ask for help. He's a sneaky sort. I didn't catch on that he was 'literate until he refused to write me a list a few times." He turned from her and headed back to the front of the room. "Then, I had to give him a few tests, and he failed." Stan paced from one side of the room to the other, glancing out every window.

He was just like Harland, controlling and cruel, but Harland had never taken leave of his senses like Stan had. She could handle someone like Harland, but would the same things work on Stan? When faced with someone stronger, better, or smarter, Harland would slink away every time. She prayed Stan would as well.

"He isn't illiterate. In fact, he can read quite well. I've listened to him."

Stan spun and faced her. "You've been fooled, girl. He's dumb as a stump and twice as wide."

She pushed against her hands tied behind her back, extricating herself from the grip of the teacher, and slid up the wall to stand. He couldn't cow her as easily if she wasn't on the floor.

"I taught him how, though he knew most everything he needed before we even began. So, how much of your plan relies on him asking for help that he won't need?" She paused to let him think about her words for a minute. "He's going to be madder than a mud hornet."

The color drained from his face for a moment. "No matter. The men will take care of anyone who tries to leave the Broken Circle O. I set plenty of them along the road. Conrad will watch his whole family die. All because he needed to ask them for help to read a simple note."

"And if they're dead, just what do you have planned for me? We are on the edge of town. People will hear you if you shoot me."

He glanced to the rafters. "Maybe I'll just get a rope. Might take five or six minutes, but you'll be quiet. Can't yell when the rope gets tight. But I need you here for now. That lout will watch you swing. I lost everything and that big, dumb fool has never lost anything!"

Isabelle tamped down the sick dread in her stomach. If she was to face death, she wouldn't let him see her fear. "I don't understand why. Why did Conrad bother you so much that you'd want to kill him, or his family? They gave you a job, a good job, which you just threw to the wind."

111

He grabbed her by the hair and yanked her back down onto the floor. "I had a ranch on the other side of town. My pa had a good plot, then the drought hit and he lost everything. I knew all there was to know about running a ranch, and I was reduced to being a wrangler for a man who couldn't even read his own deed. My pa died in shame, not owning a thing!"

Isabelle wished she'd been one of those pioneering women she'd read about from thirty or forty years before, who carried their own guns or knives. She had neither. All she had on her was her kerchief, and whatever she could find in the classroom, which wasn't much. The room hadn't been used since last Christmas, when Lula had announced to the board she couldn't continue. The poor new teacher had been inside cleaning when Stan had busted in with Isabelle over his shoulder.

Her pa and ma had come to the ranch that day, too. Now they would *certainly* want to take her away; staying was dangerous. If she made it out of the school alive...

"Ain't you got nothing to say, girl?" He laughed.

She narrowed her eyes. "I don't see any sense in talking with the likes of you. You wouldn't understand anyway. What a fool plan. You left a note so Conrad would ask for help... then you planned to have your men kill his family? Why does it matter then? Anyone who knew his secret would be dead." Did she dare to push him further?

He stopped his pacing and stared at her. "Because I want the land for myself."

Isabelle didn't know the particulars of the Oleson land, but she *did* know how to make men like Stan think. "Even if every man who could ride was killed today, you still wouldn't own it. It wouldn't be for sale. There are three women owners and one heir… and I'm not telling you who they are."

A huge group of riders rode toward town, making more clatter than Stan could ignore. He strode to the window and peered out. From where she stood, it was little more than a huge cloud of dust and riders, just a group of men coming to town. Stan yanked his gun from his holster, and Isabelle slid flat against the floor and yanked herself under the nearest row of desks, squeaking to the teacher to join her. It wouldn't stop a bullet, but he might not find her, either.

The blonde crawled to her under the tiny row of desks.

"What's your name?" Isabelle asked. "So I can pray for us."

"Stephenia. Please tell me we aren't going to die."

"I can't promise any such thing. Just hold tight to Jesus."

CHAPTER 16

H is grandpap had told him stories of the war. How you could feel the wind of a bullet as it nearly missed. He hadn't believed the stories until today. As he, Eli, Arnold, Mr. Harmon, and his pa made their way to town, they'd been set upon twice by two small groups of the cowboys they'd let go two weeks before.

The malcontents had hidden in the ditches to catch the group as they rode by, and it was only the height that sitting on a horse afforded that allowed them to see their attackers in time. The first group had been eight men, the second five. They were almost to town now, and he still had no idea where Stan might be holding Isabelle, and none of the men they'd gathered would talk.

His pa and Mr. Harmon took the group of tied vigilantes to the sheriff, and he and his brothers waited. They needed to decide their next step, or Conrad would just start riding. He had to find Isabelle, and Lord help Stan if he'd hurt her.

Arnold searched the area, his head constantly swiveling and eyes alert.

"He didn't plan for you to be able to read the note, right, Conrad?"

Conrad's jaw flexed. He didn't like that it was common knowledge in the family that he'd lacked the skill for longer than he should've. "Right."

"Well, he's probably holding her somewhere in town, at least until he hears that you've been dispatched. There are only two empty buildings available right now: the school and the place there on the main street."

Arnold was more than likely correct. Stan couldn't have kept her at his place; he stayed at the boarding house after his family had lost all their holdings a few years before. If he was keeping her in case Conrad had made it through the traps Stan had left, he'd need her safe, at least for a short time. To *trade*.

"So, my guess would be the school. It's close enough to town that he can get away and far enough out that no one will bother to look there. How do we get to it without notice?"

Eli slipped his red bandanna over his face and pulled his revolver. "We make a little noise, a little confusion, and maybe a little mess." He laughed as he spurred his mount toward the distant school.

Arnold glanced at Conrad. "Crazy Eli. You have any idea what he's got planned?"

Conrad shrugged. "If I had to guess, it'll involve getting shot at. Least we know Stan's not a good shot." He spurred his own horse after his brother.

Eli hollered, "Under fire! Open up!" as he leaned over the horse's neck and out of Stan's line of sight.

Stan slammed the door open and Conrad gripped the reins to keep from drawing and taking him out on the spot. Isabelle was somewhere inside that school, and a bullet was indiscriminate. Stan's eyes turned to great, white saucers as he realized his mistake, and he ran to get out of the way of Eli and his racing horse. Eli slapped Desperado's flank with the reins, and he ran right up the steps into the school, skidding as he slid through the double doors.

Conrad spurred his horse to follow, and Arnold was on his tail. The blast of two shots and screams from the school urged Conrad even faster, along with his heart. He slid off his mount and raced into the building. Eli's horse was against the wall and Eli knelt over someone at the front of the room. Conrad drew, just in case there was anyone else, and searched all over for Isabelle, frantic to find her.

Isabelle pushed from behind Eli's horse with her shoulder. Her hands were bound behind her and her hair was loose from its braid, but she was there. Safe. He'd found her. Arnold stopped in his tracks as he stared at the teacher, cowering on the floor. He tentatively helped the woman up, then got the shock of his life as the woman clung to him, sobbing.

Isabelle turned away from Conrad so he could cut the rope from around her wrists. He fumbled as he untied her, just wanting her in his arms.

"Is there anyone besides the teacher here we need to worry about?" He had to focus, complete the task, then he could forget about everything but his Isabelle. He'd come so close to losing her. Her cold hands trembled under his fingers.

She shook her head and the moment her hands were free, she whipped around and wrapped her arms around him. He never wanted another day to go by where he didn't feel her pressed against him. She belonged right there, in his arms. Isabelle was the woman the Lord had created just for him, and no one would ever take her from him again.

He brushed the soft, loose strands of hair out of her face and cradled her cheeks in his palms.

"I've never been more worried in all my life."

She nodded into his hands, her eyes tightly closed, and she clung to him. He let go of her face and stroked her back, hoping to calm her.

"I met your pa. He's worried about you. We'll need to go back and let him know that you're safe. Your ma, too."

He held his breath and prayed there would be no lasting harm to Isabelle. He'd never wanted to do harm to a man more than he wanted to harm Stan, with maybe the exception of Isabelle's late husband. It didn't matter that he'd tried to hurt Conrad, but once he'd hurt Isabelle, *that* he couldn't abide.

Eli glanced at him over his shoulder and shook his head, his face solemn. Stan was dead. Eli had done the job, and now he'd have to deal with the aftermath. Even if a man was aiming to kill, it was still never easy to pull the trigger.

Conrad turned Isabelle around and led her out of the building; she didn't need to see Stan any more. The sheriff would soon be there and would probably wonder why he wasn't asked to join the posse. But the work was now done, with the other men in custody, and the man in charge dead on the schoolhouse floor.

There was no better place for Isabelle than at home, but she would need to speak to the sheriff first. She'd been the one kidnapped, and *he'd* have to testify that Stan had shot at him, though he still wasn't sure if Stan had ever pulled the trigger. He'd asked one of his men to do it the first time, he may have hired it done the second time, as well. If none of the men they'd captured never spoke a word about it, they would probably never know.

The barber in Belle Fourche also happened to be the

undertaker, and he was soon brought in to take care of Stan. Conrad kept Isabelle far from where Stan lay. Though many people had become calloused to the sight of death, especially in the west, he didn't want her to have any other images from this day. She would have enough. Her wrists were red and swollen from the rope, and a gash across her face told him more than he wanted to know about her ordeal.

After the sheriff had taken her aside to ask her what she knew, they were allowed to leave. Conrad helped her mount Talon and then slid into the saddle behind her, cradling her close to his chest. Leaving her that night would be more difficult than anything he'd ever done.

CHAPTER 17

S trong arms held her. Isabelle had never felt safer, or more protected. Conrad had come for her. He was more than words, more than any man had ever been. While the ride back out to the ranch wouldn't be near long enough to enjoy the quiet freedom of soaking in Conrad's strength, she would take every moment she'd been given.

Conrad's arms tensed around her and held her even closer against him. His solid chest against her back was so reassuring. Her parents meant well, and the first year *might* be difficult, but with the right man, it would be worth fighting for.

Isabelle rested her arms over his, enjoying his embrace.

"How long will you be staying, Pa?" If he could stay for a little while, he might get to walk her down the aisle this time. Harland had married her in secret, on the way back to school. She hadn't even had anyone there to witness the occasion.

"We'll stay for a little while, as long as we're welcome."

Nathan rode closer, clicking to his horse to more easily join the conversation. He nodded and said, "You're welcome to stay as long as you need. The house is big enough." He clicked again and his horse cantered away, heading for home. The brothers and her father followed suit, leaving Conrad and Isabelle alone.

Conrad slowed the horse to a stop and let all the other riders get far ahead of them. When they were alone, he leaned slightly to the side, tracing her jaw until she turned to look at him. He looked into her eyes, and she was in awe of the emotion she found there, the love, honesty, trust, and desire.

"I want you to be my wife, Isabelle. I thought I could wait. I want you to be healed from everything you went through, both with Harland and today, but I don't want to let you go. I want you next to me. I want to know that you're safe, every day. When I get up and leave to work, I want to know that you're happy. I want to feel you curl up next to me every night. I can't let you go at the end of the day anymore. I just can't."

Isabelle tilted her head and his lips came down on hers, gentle but insistent. They both needed each other. He cradled her against his steady shoulder as she leaned back, clinging to his neck.

He caressed her face as he drew away from her. "I need to hear you say yes, Isabelle."

In her need, she'd forgotten to give him an answer. "Yes, Conrad. I'll marry you. And I'll never leave. I'll be there when you leave in the morning, and I'll be pleased to curl up next to you at night."

He tightened his hold around her waist, and her belly tightened in anticipation. She had been certain she'd never crave a man again, but Conrad had changed everything. And now, he would be there for her always.

CHAPTER 18

While his wedding was only a few hours away, he couldn't stay away from his bride, who was stuck in the kitchen making rolls for her own wedding. As he ducked through the back door, expecting her to be in a foul temper, her humming and dancing around the kitchen took him off guard.

"Well, aren't you in pleasant spirits?" he caught her about the waist as she waltzed by him.

She laughed. "Why wouldn't I be? In a few hours, I will have the husband I've always wanted, a new home, and a purpose."

He gently kissed her nose. "You had a purpose before, but I sure am glad I'm the focus of it now."

He slipped a paper from his vest pocket and handed it to her.

"You'll have to read it; my hands are sticky." She grinned at him. How he loved that smile.

"I don't have to read it. I read it before I signed it. It's the legal certificate that says we can get married this afternoon. Once you sign it, it's legal."

Heat rushed to Isabelle's cheeks. He'd never tire of seeing that pretty pink.

He still couldn't fathom how this beautiful, intelligent woman would ever want anything to do with him. "Are you glad you chose to come to Belle Fourche, Isabelle? What if you lose interest…?"

She shook her head and smiled. "I'm so glad I came. And you'll have to tie me to a runaway horse to get rid of me. And I know you'll keep me busy until I don't know what to do."

He prayed it wasn't just him that kept her busy, but the baby she wanted so very much. That they both wanted. He'd never even thought about children until Isabelle. Now, they wanted to fill his small home to bursting with them.

Isabelle's mother and father strode into the kitchen. "Conrad Oleson, you get out of here! Don't you know it's bad luck to see your bride before the wedding?"

He hadn't known, and it wouldn't have mattered. He wanted to see her no matter what. He scooped her close and ran his finger over her lip, testing its softness. Her gaze found his and kindled a lightning-hot fire in him that only she could tame. He bent and kissed her lips gently, tasting the cinnamon from where she'd tested her confections earlier. He waited to feel her pull closer to him, to draw him nearer to her. How he loved that she hungered for him as much as he for her. As he drew away, Mrs. Harmon threw a tea towel at him.

"Now, get out!"

He laughed. "Yes, ma'am!" To his bride he whispered, "Soon, my love."

⁓

ISABELLE LOVED HER PARENTS, but she hadn't wanted to talk to either of them. The wound was still too fresh. Her mother had chosen to believe a lie rather than her own daughter. Tension in the kitchen built now that they were alone.

"Izzy, your ma and I, we were so worried about you when we got your letter. We didn't know what you were thinking, running off to Belle Fourche instead of coming home. Thought you might be out of your mind with grief. Your ma, she was torn clean apart by your letter." He put his arm around his wife in support. "Harland acted like he was so good to you, he always made it sound like he was taking good care of you." Her pa shook his head. "I can't believe we didn't see it."

They had refused to see it, but she wouldn't dwell on the past. Harland was gone, and she never wanted to be alone again. Her parents could be forgiven, they had seen so little of what had happened, and Harland had been a good liar.

"We both talked with Mr. and Mrs. Oleson about Conrad, something that we never did with Harland. We just took his word when he said he was in love with you and wanted to spend his life with you. He looked like he would have a good job, and we trusted him."

Ma stepped forward. "Your father and I will be leaving tomorrow. There's no real reason for us to stay any longer."

Isabelle wiped her hands on her apron. While it wasn't her mother's fault she'd married that fool, she had been the driving force that kept her there. If not for her mother's chastising words, she would've left Harland. Begged to stay with them. If her mother had allowed her to come back home, she never would've lost the baby... because it never would've been planted to begin with.

"I know now my advice was wrong, but what else could I say? You were a married woman. We had no idea he would wed you so quickly. We thought he'd wait until the end of the school term, since you were already through half of the year."

Isabelle didn't want to hear excuses for *why* anymore. Her heart was too full of Conrad to ever let Harland take back even a bird's portion.

"Mother, it's done. Over. I tried to get you to listen to me through my letters, but I know that I was not plain enough in my speaking for you to understand what life was truly like. And I couldn't explain any further for fear he would somehow find my letters. There was a time I even feared that you would tell him. You see me now, how I am after weeks of being cared for by Maretta and Conrad. You didn't see the waif that came here, running because she had nowhere to go."

"We would've taken you in. You're a widow, Izzy." Her mother stepped forward and reached for her.

While Isabelle wanted to forgive, was trying so hard to forget, she couldn't accept her mother's affection yet. She stepped out of reach. It was difficult not to seat blame for the loss of her child just as much in her mother's lap as Harland's.

"You would've taken me in? Perhaps, but you wouldn't have listened. You still didn't want to believe what I wrote to you until you thought I was in danger and you were worried you might never see me again. Pain will bring out the truth."

Ma rested her hands on the counter. They were strong, callused hands, which had raised seven boys and one girl. Only now was she finally allowing herself to slow down a bit and let her boys and their wives do the work.

"We believe you now, isn't that what matters?" she whispered.

"It's a start." Isabelle pulled the finished rolls from the oven and left them on the counter to cool. "Excuse me. I need to go get ready for my wedding. I'm glad that you can stay, and you and Pa are welcome here any time you want to visit. But today, I refuse to bring up the past. I don't want to remember a single moment of it. Conrad is better on his worst day than Harland was on his very best, and I refuse to examine my mistakes anymore."

Her pa sighed heavily. "I know Conrad's parents would probably tend to give him a glowing report, but they were honest. You don't need our blessing; you're a woman full-grown. But if you care to have our blessing, you have it."

A slight peace rested over her shoulders. Not only could she be with Conrad, she could reach out to her parents once again when she was ready. The hole left in their absence slowly filled.

"Thank you. That does mean a lot. I was so worried you'd never accept me again. That... you loved Harland more than me."

"You're our daughter. That could never happen. We knew you were unhappy, but many wives are at first. Married life isn't like the life of a child, without responsibility."

Isabelle bristled at the reminder. She'd barely been an adult when she'd said her vows but had been forced to grow up quickly. "Your time to council has come too late." Every word her parents said would now be examined for its meaning. They hadn't cared about her for far too long.

"You won't be coming to visit us, will you?" Ma wrapped her arms around her waist, her shoulders hunched and her expression haggard.

"No. Conrad runs this ranch, and I don't see us leaving for any length of time." And she wouldn't voluntarily leave him. Not ever.

CHAPTER 19

Maretta strode into Isabelle's shop, a basket on her arm and a bright smile on her face.

"Isabelle! Before you close up shop, I need some of those rolls Nathan likes so much. If we hurry, we can even beat Conrad. He'll be in in just a minute."

As she pushed open the gleaming case that displayed her sweet rolls, she could hardly contain her excitement. She'd been thinking about him all day. Maretta rarely came into town with Conrad, and now, since there was someone else, Isabelle would have to wait a little longer to speak to him, but no matter. She'd been expectant for the ride home, but they would have the rest of their lives to steal a few quiet moments alone.

Conrad strode through the door. Even after they'd been married for three months, just seeing him made her heart race. He drove her in to the bakery every morning, and picked her up every evening, never complaining about how far it was. They had yet to discuss the winter, and if she'd still come in or not, but she wouldn't fight with him. The bakery was only to keep her busy until she would be needed at home. Her hand pressed her belly for just a moment, and a sigh escaped her.

He looked up over her head at the new menu she'd written on the chalkboard and hitched an eyebrow. She could almost laugh. His gaze slid back down to hers as he chuckled.

"I'll take a half dozen of whatever 'Conrad's favorite' is. Sounds pretty good."

Isabelle handed Maretta's bag to her and then opened another, putting six huge, sticky cinnamon rolls inside.

"I should've known. I can't get enough of those." Conrad leaned over the counter. "And there's something else back here I can't quite get enough of…" She met his lips over the counter and gave him a little of her own favorite kind of sugar.

Maretta cleared her throat. "Now, you two. We're in the middle of town. Save that for at home."

Conrad opened the little flip up counter that separated her from the front of the store and took her hand as she neared him.

"Time to go, my sweet?"

She smiled at the man she loved more than anyone in the world and nodded as she followed his lead. Tonight would be the best evening they'd ever had because, while she'd been rolling dough that morning, her head had been figuring some things. And if she'd figured correctly, in late April or early May, they would welcome the next little Oleson to the family.

DID YOU LOVE THE STORY? Would you like the next? Not sure? Read on for chapter one of, *What the Heart Holds*.

WHAT THE HEART HOLDS

Brothers of Belle Fourche: Book 2

CHAPTER 1

Belle Fourche, South Dakota
September, 1899

Arnold stretched his legs in his stirrups, raising himself to see better, and stared over the rolling green hills at the road leading to the one-room schoolhouse, then clenched his jaw as an unfamiliar worry settled in his gut. School would start today, not that a man of twenty and eight should care. But this would be the first day in months the teacher at the little Belle Fourche schoolhouse would let him be. At least for a while. Once the children got out of class, he wasn't so sure. Still, it would be best to keep watch for the glint of her blonde hair in the sun.

He'd always managed to catch her far off, near the road, so his parents didn't know she came out to see him. She was so young—*too* young—and well, he just wasn't sure about anything except that he'd rather she didn't visit at all.

Behind him, Conrad cleared his throat. Arnold shifted in the saddle to glance at his taller—though in every other way almost identical to himself—brother.

"You going to watch the road, or the cattle as they scatter farther away? I could always go get Eli if you'd rather ride into town to give your girl a flower or something."

Arnold grit his teeth. His brother could joke all he wanted. *He* was married, safe from the attentions of well-meaning, but far too ambitious, teachers. Blowing out a breath, Arnold turned and faced Conrad. "I'm ready."

His brother laughed. "She wouldn't come out now anyway unless she quit her teaching job, hoping you'd come to your senses."

Arnold held in a groan. He'd been worried about that very thing. She was nothing if not persistent. Stephenia, or Miss Forde as the children called her, was under the false impression that he'd saved her life. A fact he'd tried to correct every chance he got.

Conrad quirked a brow. "You know, some other cowboy is going to march into that schoolhouse and give that pretty teacher an apple. You just wait. She won't seem half bad when she isn't chasing you anymore."

Arnold frowned and settled himself back in the saddle, ready for more working with cattle and less talking about the teacher. His brother only knew about Miss Forde's visits because he'd happened to see her one day on her way up the drive. Even though Arnold never invited her to the house, she didn't seem to lose heart. Conrad had given him the once over for that, too. But he couldn't have Ma getting her hopes up. He wasn't going to marry, and a woman coming around would only cause problems.

He fingered the red bandanna he wore as a reminder that love and life were fleeting. "I would gladly set her up with Eli or anyone else. I don't need a woman."

Conrad gathered one end of his reins and whipped his leg

with it. "Lynellen wouldn't want you to sit here rotting, Arnold. Stop acting like you don't deserve to live."

Lynellen. The name punched Arnold in the gut. She was his first and only love.

Rage burned white hot, curling his hands into fists. "She didn't deserve to die, so why should I just move on like nothing happened?"

Conrad turned his mount west to the pasture and left without answering—because there was no answer.

Arnold yanked the red bandanna Lynellen had given him up over his face and kicked Desperado to a gallop. Even now, years after losing her, he still couldn't let go.

Because if he did, she might be gone forever.

STEPHENIA STARED out the schoolroom window, mulling over the three things she'd learned in the last few months as the new teacher in the little Belle Fourche school: local people would tease good-naturedly if you pronounced the silent *r* in the name of the town, the sound and smell of the stockyard and railroad could never fully be ignored, and Arnold Oleson was probably the most amazing man that ever lived. Though her current distraction was almost solely Arnold.

Pulling her gaze from the window, she tried to focus on the students, sitting in their neat rows, girls on one side and boys on the other. The tidy blue painted cheery interior with a little cloak hall in the back of the room should've been enough to keep her interest, especially because teaching was what she'd wanted to do since she'd learned to read. Luckily it was the first day of a new school year and the children were as antsy to get it over with as she was. Her pocket watch felt heavy attached at her waist, but she wouldn't look at it again. At least not until she was sure a minimum of ten minutes had passed.

"Miss Forde?" Carmine, a young girl of about nine, raised her hand.

"Yes, dear?" She hid a grimace. How many times must she tell herself to stop calling the children by anything but their names so she'd learn them quicker?

"Miss Forde, why is there a gunshot hole to the right of the blackboard there? That wasn't there last year."

She didn't turn to look, but she didn't need to. She knew it by heart. The shot had happened last summer, the very day she'd met Arnold Oleson. The day he'd saved her life...and changed it. He was the most handsome man she'd ever set eyes on. He had sandy hair and blue eyes that some would call hard—*she* would call them strong—capable shoulders, a firm jaw and he was tall enough that she had to tip her head just so to look him in the eye.

She smiled at the girl. "There was an accident in the school building last summer, but no matter. It will be patched up before winter."

At least she hoped it would be. She'd asked the school board, but summer was a busy time for them, even the ones who lived in town. Fall was harvest and even now, they wouldn't see some of the older boys for a few weeks. Somehow, when she'd planned to become a teacher, these things had escaped her, how she'd have to collect work for the older boys. Her own family had been huge, nine children born and three that survived to marry.

"I hope no one was hurt," a little boy piped up from the front row. Stephenia couldn't remember his name to remind him not to talk out of turn.

Someone *had* been hurt, killed in fact, the one who'd held

her and Isabelle Oleson captive—though she'd been Isabelle Lawson then.

She shoved the horrid memory away and reached for a small slate on her desk. "It's of no concern right now. Let's practice our math facts." She held up her board to demonstrate. "I would like the younger grades to practice addition facts, middle grades should do multiplication, and the older grades may work on division. Go."

That would keep them busy for another few minutes. Setting the board back on her desk, she glanced out the window one more time. Belle Fourche sat a few blocks distant from the school, and it was a bustling cow town. The Cheyenne River ran right along the edge, but even though the town was named because of the river, it was known most for its cowboys. Talented men who could rope, ride, and brand. Strong men. But she didn't care a whit for any but one. She frowned. And that one couldn't possibly want her around any less.

It really was for the best. She'd planned to never marry, to act as a daily mother to all her students so she wouldn't feel the heartache of loss like her own mother. Her heart sank just thinking about her past and Arnold. The more she tried to get his attention, the more he withdrew.

She'd been told she was pretty, with her blonde hair, brown eyes, straight nose and cheeks that made her look happy most times. But she was beginning to think all those who'd spoken of her beauty were lying. Obviously, her looks weren't enough to turn *his* head.

As the little faces popped up, finished with their work, and stared at her, she chanced one last look at her pocket watch and decided to call it a day. "Class, once you've finished, you may pack your things and be done. Please don't dawdle around the yard today. Head on home." Because she wouldn't be around long to watch them.

A smile twitched her lips. Arnold Oleson might not want to see her, but she couldn't stop herself from going out to visit him. Not even when she shouldn't, late on a school day.

ALSO BY KARI TRUMBO

Get the sequel to Teach Me To Love,

What the Heart Holds, now.

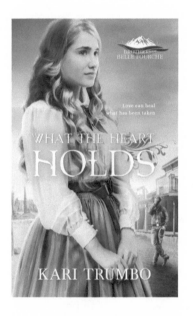

A review helps me know what you want to read next.

Visit your favorite online retailer to let me know.

Looking for a novel length romance?

Try An Imperfect Promise

ABOUT THE AUTHOR

Kari Trumbo is an International bestselling author of Christian and sweet romance. She writes swooney heroes and places that become characters, with historical detail and heart.

She's a stay-at-home mom to four vibrant children. When she isn't writing, reading, or editing, she home schools her children and pretends to keep up with them.

She makes her home in Central Minnesota—land of frigid toes and mosquitoes the size of compact cars—with her husband of over twenty years, two daughters, two sons, two cats, and one hungry wood stove.

facebook.com/KariTrumboAuthor
twitter.com/KariTrumbo
bookbub.com/authors/kari-trumbo

Made in United States
Troutdale, OR
10/27/2023